A Moment of Doubt

JIM NISBET

A Moment of Doubt
Jim Nisbet
© Jim Nisbet

This edition © PM Press 2010. All rights reserved. No
part of this book may be transmitted by any means
without permission in writing from the publisher.

ISBN: 978-1-60486-307-9
Library of Congress Control Number: 2010927771

Cover art by Gent Sturgeon
Cover layout by John Yates
Interior design by briandesign

10 9 8 7 6 5 4 3 2 1

PM Press
PO Box 23912
Oakland, CA 94623
www.pmpress.org

The Green Arcade
1680 Market Street
San Francisco, CA 94102-5949
www.thegreenarcade.com

Printed in the USA on recycled paper.

By the same author:

Kordeschore to Jack Hirschman for permission to use *Peacedove*.
CP/M and its utilities are registered
trademarks of Digital Research.
The version of "HELLO.ASM" reproduced herein
originally appeared in *CP/M Revealed*, by Jack D. Denon.
Thanks to John and Stephanie for their *juratorii ab riso*;
to Henry for analogue legwork *vis a vis* Erich Heckel;
to Michael and George for assiduous downloading;
to David, for having the nerve;
and a free tastebudectomy to Kevin Killian.

O N E

... some kind of ultimate solipsism, big words and a hope-less attitude holding a needle gleaming with pre-ejac-ulatory fluid over the bent elbow bulging with circula-tion-deprived veins beyond the greasy thick hand-tooled leather belt with rising-sun-of-optimism belt buckle and the rolled sleeve. Black, too. Black sleeve. But needle work gives chickenshits like me the hyperventilations. The sweat come out cold already on your face. The point shiv-ers above a weak flesh that's screaming no to the rest of its system, its so-called friends, No, no, can't you see what it's trying to do to me? To you? To us? But the system doesn't listen, at least the listening part of it doesn't listen. Certain nerves duck into a bar for a quick shot. Others prepare some of that precipitate sociology folk like to come up with at times like this. Like, just imagine, if you can get your mind off that pre-ejaculatory fluid gleaming at the tip of the quivering needle, just imagine the pressure on this poor slob if he's driven himself to this, the extreme of puncturing his own skin with a steel sliver, let alone the injection that follows, of a thick, mean fluid worse than any come that was ever shot, and purer, too, I'm straying, by man or beast or poly-dicked alien whoremonger, such extremes deep in the thick, bullshit encrusted sociological palimpsest labeled "Facial Distortions Encountered on Street Shitheads Due to the Tremendous Societal G-Forces Exerted Over the Mauled Extrapyramidal Features by His Scumbag Peer Group," by One Who Knows.

It's hard, here, not to quote chapter and verse. Bob Dylan and Faulkner cornered the Bible. Fitzgerald bled Keats completely dry—although he never named one of his books *Alien Corn*, though he should have; Hemingway sacked Donne; Shakespeare did Shakespeare. Although nobody, until now, has utilized *Toys of Desperation*. Since this is the computer generation, I'm going to rename this book, called *SCRAM*, rename it *Toys of Desperation*, using the simple REN utility supplied with every copy of CP/M. Ready?

`REN B:`

(since we're on the A: drive)

`REN B:TOYSDESP=SCRAM<cr>`

Kapow! Bet you didn't even feel it. Check the cover. Different? You betcha. Check this one out.

`REN B:SCRAM=TOYSDESP<cr>`

Now what's it say? *A Moment of Doubt*? Imagine that. Hold on. Which do you prefer?

`If SCRAM enter 0:`

`If TOYS OF DESPERATION enter 1:`

Now check the cover. Like it? Yes? Good. No trace of either? Tricky. Tricky, that is, unless you got what it takes to use a disassembler, a debugging utility, a reassembler, etc., etc., to alter this program, this book you're holding, by yourself. I'll even give you a hint, dear reader: right now, right this very moment, as you're buying, holding, reading, thinking about this text, you're deep, deep within a SUBMIT routine, conceived, written, and implemented a long, long time ago, by me. Your dear chickenshit author. And as of now, because you found out about all this too late, you're lucky I'm benevolent. Consider.

Tiny's pants split along the length of his member, the buttons popped loose like rivets exploding out of a submarine lost in the Mariana Trench. His dick looked like a road map wrapped around a blackjack drawn by S. Clay Wilson. XYX chromosomes, jaundiced corpuscles, cocaine and heroin coursed through thick veins the size of garden hoses up and around it like multilevel twinight freeways pulsing light around a skyscraper in a future megalopolis, like molten hydrogen in transparent conduits up and down a launchable, scum-charged rocket. Tiny encircled this inter-disciplinary vehicle with a thick thumb and forefinger and milked its root with a violent twist. A pearl of pre-ejaculatory fluid described a path through the foetid air of the dimly lit room like a sparkler flung off a bridge into a septic canal in some nameless, hopeless European city on a dark night full of murdered whores, to the wine-stained, cat-spattered 'carpet' below.

"Indeed," the voice of the third man only added to the darkness, "that marvelous prick's not unlike a ray of hope in an otherwise hopeless city of doom." He paused in order to exhale the pungent smoke of his perennial, unfiltered Gitane into the dank air between them. "Wouldn't you say, Mr. Windrow?"

Windrow said nothing.

The slim hoodlum aimed the point of one of his impeccable lovely Italian shoes at the pit of Windrow's stomach, betraying his taste for melodrama. But he missed. A little high. Windrow heard the rib, one well known to him, the 'floater', *so-called because, unlike the ones above it, the floater is not attached to the sternum, crack. He felt it, too. Both sensations were duly reported to that cortical emissary in charge of such things, who sent a 'groan' message through channels. Windrow groaned. Then he drooled on himself, as the so-called 'black wing' passed momentarily before his eyes. Tiny made the sort of sound in his throat most people associate with pleasure, and slid his fist slowly up the entire length of his immense cock.*

Feel safe? Wet? Erect? Yeah. Yeah! And why? What do you know of these people? What's their motivation, there are three of them, for Chrissakes! Where is this room, with come on the walls? Why don't we all have a key to it, if they ever lock it? But why would they lock it? Who the hell would want to get in here? *Youse do?*

"Tiny, here, has AIDS, Mr. Windrow." The man known as Thimbelina viciously grabbed a handful of Windrow's hair and yanked the groaning detective's head up. Why can't you let him alone, the cortical emissary frowned, he's given himself up to the moans already, they're good for him, and they're what you want, aren't they? But Thimbelina was adamant, he had something else on his mind. "Can you hear me? Are you listening, Mr. Windrow?" Someone beyond the window and three stories down on a busy street stood on their horn impatiently. Thimbelina threw Windrow's head aside as if it were the wadded up brown paper bag the second six pack had arrived in. "Gleam of sapience," Thimbelina muttered, staring out the window to Eddy Street below.

'Gleam of sapience.' That's a good one. How could anyone allow my dimwitted detective to be compared to an amber bead of pitch on a board?

He exhaled smoke against the glass. Whores, beggars, a couple of socialites getting out of a black limousine, lots of traffic including the cab blaring its horn backed up behind it, two cops talking to two hookers in a doorway, the hookers smoking and smiling nervously, these guys wanta chat or fuck or pop or what, the cops smiling in their moment of power for the evening, and Thimbelina puts out his butt against the glass between them and him, grinds the cinders slowly against the transparency, the dead ashes sift onto the sill below, he doesn't like cops.

"Tiny's very horny, Mr. Windrow," says he, absently, "very horny indeed." The thin man turned from the window and considered the dark room. Windrow was trussed to a chair, leaning away from the electrical cords torn from the overturned television set, that bound him to the chair, leaning away from his bonds and into his pain. Tiny stood very near Windrow, not close enough to touch the detective, but close enough to excite himself, against the wall beyond the foot of the bed.

"I, personally," continued Thimbelina, crossing the room, "would love to oblige him—have, in fact, done so, in the past," he added wistfully, "but, alas, no longer can we indulge our ... passion." Saying this, Thimbelina stroked Tiny's immense engine with the long, carefully manicured nail of his delicate forefinger. "Oh," Thimbelina said breathlessly, "we continue to tease one another, that doesn't matter." He turned his back on the hulking Tiny and faced Windrow, who regarded this soliloquy obliquely with one eye, squinting through his pain. "It's the so-called blood contact that does you in." He crossed back to the window and considered the world through it. Rain had begun to fall against the pane. Thimbelina made as if to touch one of the raindrops though the glass. "Diseased come in your ass is what they're talking about when they say that," he murmured, following the raindrop with his fingernail as it progressed down the glass, toward the cheap aluminum frame below. But

*the nail's pace accelerated, leaving the drop behind, until the
cuticle suddenly screeched down to the sill and halfway back
up. The sharp, jagged sound penetrated even Windrow's pain
and made his spine shiver. Tiny, three hundred pounds if he
was an ounce, groaned deep in his throat, stood up on his toes,
arched his pelvis in the air before him, and extended his fist
along the length of his penis until the clubbed head of it disap-
peared beneath the fold between his chubby thumb and forefinger. These digits then tested the fluid squeezed thus out of
the tip of his urethra as if it were a precious liquor possessing
a fantastic index of viscosity, which it is and does, then slid it
all back down the length of his cock and smeared his balls and
crotch with it, his pants meanwhile dropping to his knees.*

*"Epic, isn't it, Mr. Windrow?" Thimbelina had turned to
appraise the scenario of his own creation again. "A beautiful thing, wasted now, soon to be . . ." He turned again to the
window. Tiny, staring at Windrow, began to use his free hand
to play with his own ass.*

I can't take it anymore, either, and pace out to the mail-
box. Several of my subscriptions have expired. A check,
overdue for six months, arrives miraculously. This will
allow me to survive for another week, if I don't pay the
rent, which has been due for three weeks. I hate to do this
to my landlady. She's a doll and would probably allow me
to fuck her for a discount, perhaps for the whole thing.
She doesn't even need the money. But she owns my home,
what can I do but put up with her conditions? A catalog
for gardening tools, and a flyer inquiring after a lost child.
Actually, she'd love to throw me out because she's read my
last couple of detective novels, but she's afraid to do so
for the same reason. Someone stupidly gave them to her
as 'light' entertainment during one of her periodic trips
to Club Med. About a week later she remembered where

she'd seen the name before. All those checks! Month after month, for years! She'd no idea she's harboring an artist, she thought I was just a bum. Wait till she realizes the difference. She's begun to get the idea already, by getting me to autograph certain pages of *So Long, Pockface*, detailing in some detail a rather arcane codex to the Kama Sutra made up entirely out of my imagination. She thought she knew that book backwards and forwards, as it were, the Kama Sutra I mean. She has taken, it seems, the trouble to know my books backwards and forwards, at least it would seem so by the way she quotes them to me and makes coy little references to events and remarks in them, but most of these naturally go right over my head, since she obviously knows the books very well, much better than I, at least, know them. She could let on to me about the page numbers of purple-assed baboons in bondage, coyly, and I'd be none the wiser. I try to make the books interesting, to a certain cut of mind, but I can't be expected to remember how or why I have done so in the past. It's hit or miss anyway, so far as I'm concerned. Usually I just try to write dreamy, with lots of knives and forks and trains and assholes and stuff, so that it seems a certain kind of inevitability is involved, an inexorable kind of plant life is growing up between the words as you read them, or as you leave them in the dark, folded against one another, behind you as you go, so that, even as you refer backwards to a passage you've already read, to clarify the one you're reading now, the older one seems unrecognizable as you reread it, and you can't reconcile what's on the page in front of you with your own until now very clear memory of it, which after all was just installed there moments or at the most a few days before, while you were on the A train ignoring the fat lady, blind, with a stick and a cup in one hand, groping the air in front of her with the other, making her way up the car singing "Over the Rainbow," in the most plaintive voice you've ever heard, the crustiest New Yorkers dropping coins in her cup. It's like the first time you ever heard Judy Garland sing the tune, knowing she was fucked up on pills already and slated to die a horrible death in between the recording and your audition of it, while you were still suckling papaya juice in a childhood island paradise, hopelessly ignorant of the ways and steel teeth and leafy humid dick-shaped tendrils of the world. *Vagina dentata*, let's don't forget all that, too, Kama Sutra, while we're at it. That's the kind of writing I try to do.

Of course, the simpler you keep it, the better off you are. But no matter how you feel about it, you always want to emend, amend, interlineate, stipulate, regrind, make corollaries, footnote, restart, delete, and generally inflate your original train of thought.

"It's not unlike having a giant turbine carefully wrapped in your colon, Mr. Windrow, with all of the Hoover Dam coping with all of the snowmelt of the springtime Sierra Nevada coursing through it, and your prostate lights up like the city of Las Vegas, and your balls tingle like Tijuana next to it, and you recreate the river, plunging through the tubes, into the gorge below . . ."

You can't imagine how many times I've slaved over that passage. Tweaking it, stuffing it, charging it with emotion, meaning, sex . . . I type almost as fast as I lie, about 90 words a minute . . . . It's hard, it's a bitch concentrating on this stuff, especially the first time through, especially with the landlady breezing in and out all the time in her diaphanous kimono, buttonless, sashless, undergarmentless, her hair just so, lips wet and slightly parted, you can't miss them, especially when you're on the john in the little closet at the end of the hall, reading a computer magazine, and in she comes, there's only one way to get from the hallway to the bathtub in the next room, and that's through the john. So she's always, it seems, just going in to have a bath, and you somehow forgot to shoot the bolt in the door, or just stepping out of the bath, wet and fresh, hair up in a towel, another wrapped around her. The second towel always covers her breasts very well, she's shy about them, though I personally think they're magnificent … Restif de la Bretonne declared a woman's breasts as proof for the existence of God and I believe him … But the bottom of the towel never quite does the job. It stops midway along the cheeks of her ass, even when she's standing in front of me and leaning back, trying to pull the hem down over her buns, excusing herself to me for interrupting me in the 'library', as she calls it, seeing as how every time she does this I'm trying to get some reading done, and squeezing past me toward the hall door. This is no easy feat. She has to step over me, sitting on the john with my pants around my ankles, over my knees to get in between me and the hall door, which of course opens inward, awkward. Naturally, she's tall. And always, always she gets wedged between the door and my face, so that, the eighth or ninth time this happened, instead of excusing myself and blushing and absentmindedly standing up and leaning back against the toilet tank, knocking all the old copies of *Reader's Digest* stacked on top of it to the floor, so that she could see damn well I had this immense hardon, the eighth or ninth time I say, I just sat there, just sat there, and stared at this clean, damp, silken bush not one inch from my nose. I could smell her, I could practically taste her. She's dragging the towel down to cover her ass and making all these flustered excuses, so that the front of the towel actually picks up and droops down onto the top of my head, I'm surrounded by her smells and her textiles, so that, still reading the computer magazine in my left hand, I put my right finger up her slippery, tight cunt, and thumb her clitoris. Isaac Newton discovered gravity, right?

Her breath hisses past her teeth. It sounds like a case of whiskey sliding across the countertop at the liquor store, New Year's Eve, paid for. Good whiskey. Noting my place in the article on CP/M utilities, I manipulate her labia. She moves her hips elliptically, suggestive. The penis, throwing off its downcast attitude, leaps up past the rim of the toilet, almost tearing off the prepuce on the bottom edge of the seat. It stands there, lurid, colorful and erect. It looks like Coit Tower at Christmastime, or most other municipally festive monuments, for that matter, at that time of the year. Think of the Empire State Building, the Sears Tower, the Washington Monument, Le Tour Eiffel, the Leaning Tower of Pisa, think of the Master Builder high atop the scaffold dropping the wreath over the tip of his spire and try not to laugh, go ahead, this is the twentieth century, go ahead. I'm busy. Marlene—you might as well know her name, she frequently has rooms to let—right away Marlene has her tongue rimming the lips of her open mouth and her breath coming and going like a beautiful apoplectic executive's, jogging up the Kearney steps with a hangover, one hand gripping the doorknob and the other buried in a fistful of my hair. She clutches my mouth to her cunt and begs me to suck. Lick, suck, please, she said. The towel opens along an inverted V up her side and falls off as she places one of her large, highly arched, beautifully veined, perfectly formed feet on the toilet tank behind me, to facilitate the advantage I already have of being slightly beneath her, so that, looking up, I have this vision of a purplish-pink, steaming, smoking, dripping, paradisical garden, hung all round by dusky damp tendrils of mercy and passion, which is what any good optimist should see when he looks up, to heaven, but rarely does.

She clutches my face to her cunt and it's time to go to work. Rain begins to fall on the roof. Marlene screams for no apparent reason. I play a game, like mumble-de-peg or backgammon or any of those stupid frolics kids waste their time on, with pegs and holes, or parking attendants with slots and cars. The finger goes in her asshole, the thumb in her cunt, and my tongue finds her clitoris. The latter is presented to the teeth for little nips. She hisses and howls. My hand and face are soaked. A telephone rings down the hall. The doorbell chimes simultaneously. The rain increases. Now she has both her hands full of my hair, and rubs my skull against her crotch like she's grating cheese. I roll the folded computer magazine into the kerf of her ass and tilt it in and out of the juices now so copiously flooding my hand, my face, her thighs. I riffle the pages like a deck of cards against her anus. With a shout she stumbles against the door and the frosted glass rattles in its sash, her foot slips off the toilet tank and hits the handle. The john flushes with a roar, and her screams announce her orgasm over the sound of the rushing waters with the combined terror and adrenaline of all the assholes who ever threw themselves over Niagara Falls in barrels. I am wrested off the toilet and into the wall with a crash, my head and shoulders jammed in between the bowl and the paper roll, down to the floor, still gnawing away, all my knuckles buried in her streaming orifices, her ass clutched to my face, gasping for air, for life, for meaning itself, where there is little or none, but more than most places.

But wait. She's found my cock. My hips are over the bowl and I'm upside down head first into a pile of *Reader's Digests* with asswipe unrolling into my face. But she's standing over me with this incredible leer on her face, her lips distorted into a Mardi Gras of lust, the blood teeming beneath her features, her lips swollen, her cheeks inflamed, my balls in her hands. She turns and bends over my cock and sets to work. She takes the whole thing into her mouth, its head rings her epiglottis like a test of strength in a carnival, we can both feel it, my balls heatedly throwing on a load of come like ten frantic sweating eight-armed Martians filling ten eight-doored baggage cars with huge sacks of letters with eight stamps written by octillions of people .... Her teeth drag off a layer of molecules on its way out. I howl in pain and pleasure— which is which? The rain is pouring on the roof now, the doorbell, audible throughout the four-story house, rings loud and long. People next door and on the street probably think someone's getting murdered in here, and they're right in a way, somebody is getting murdered here, in a parallel universe, underneath a computer magazine on my desk, somebody has to be getting murdered, it's absolutely necessary, this thing has gone on for too long, for pages already, without so much as an iota of gore, kill now, stupid, now, kill before it's too late, kill before they notice you can't write, or that they can't read, or that their dicks are hard and they're on a bus where everyone can see and they're too weak to be buying and transporting this kind of trash because they can't stop themselves from reading it and getting hardons on buses because, after all, it's so fucking long between stops ....

My load chokes her, and if she dies, I can stop writing for the day. She makes that wonderful sound you frequently hear in bars, when some Perrier goes down the wrong way. The trouble with the cricoid. Good title for a medical thriller. But she's an animal, her natural voracity overcomes the mere mechanics of the situation, by sheer desire and talent and uninhibited abandon she is able to warp the plumbing into the fulfillment of her lust. As a result, still the come comes. She's opened a direct conduit from my balls to her tonsils, and it's like her tonsils are singing in the shower, turning in it, cupping their little hands up to the flow, directing it toward their faces, their breasts, their cunts—they're teenaged twin sisters—their hair, their necks, presenting their lovely long perfectly curved throats to it, bathing, exulting, lavishly reveling in the preposterous, opulent, hot supply of fresh, high-pressure, municipal sperm, on the planet Spermola.

I discover I've been shouting a bit myself. Two stories below people are pounding on the door and frantically ringing the doorbell. You'd think they'd be used to this sort of thing by now. But people who don't fuck all the time have no imagination, and no standard of comparison. Above me hovers the most fuckable asshole I've seen in a long time. It looks like the Masonic eye, radiating from atop a pyramid formed by two white, smooth thighs, it looks like an energy portal to another high-energy universe, a place where entropy is more than just a way of life, capable of sucking in everything that gets near it, particularly my cock, if I could get it up again, but likely also everything else in the room, the toilet paper, the *Reader's Digests*, the computer magazine, the five or six bits of change that have fallen out of my jeans onto the toilet tank, the floor, and into the bowl itself. Marlene's busy licking my balls, getting physical, cooing over what they've just done like good little students. And I'm gazing up at her lovely asshole like it's Halley's comet and I'm Halley, or it's Juliet's balcony and I'm Romeo, etc., only marginally aware that my back's killing me, or that the neighbors have begun to batter the front door down, or that I've managed to pass the last few moments quite content to live with the fact that I've not killed anyone yet today, and may not get around to it . . . .

T W O

I've spilled heroin all over the computer. This could be bad news for the disk drives, they're kind of touchy, especially these older jobs, caked as they are with all the sleaze I've sent through them over the years. I'll clean them with coke to wake them up. Sleep mode, coke mode, smack mode, speedball mode, the drives get it all, they deserve hits of each and the best, considering what they go through, what goes through them. My two disc drives, they're like priests in twin confessionals, with a single supplicant, slobbering and masturbating and retailing sin after sin, alternating between them, so each has time to digest the horror, the insanity, the lust, the gore, the needle marks on the spines of my books, the incredibly labyrinthine descriptions of my landlady's vagina, and what brandy tastes like when it's sipped from there, and speculations about how the unction of the Holy Sacrament might better serve mankind, were it dispensed from Marlene's cunt—we're hawking extreme unction. My God, one of these priests would say, and getting a faraway expression in his eye, as if in his mind racing to an astral file in heaven to check up on precedents, he commences to grind away at this idea, just like a disc drive gone off to look for something it hasn't already loaded into RAM, caught by surprise that you'd be bringing up such a thing now, laddie, as sipping the sacramental wine out of a lady's vagina, and, now, he ponders, forefinger by his swollen Irish nose, would that be in an *upright* position, or . . .

Check you later, Fadder, call me if you get an insight. I've got to go, it's Tuesday already, there's heroin all over the computer, and I haven't killed enough people yet this week to pay for it.

But it's not that simple. Nothing's ever easy in this life. By the time I make it back to my room, with a hand-ful of change, holding up my pants and trying to find my place in the computer magazine, I'm so distracted by the possibility of having to commit murder in the midst of an otherwise more or less numinous day that I only absently run my finger through the smack on the chassis, wondering where this umber dust came from, and look-ing up at the ceiling above the machine like a goddamn idiot, that I forget to realize that the shit has materialized out of nowhere, out the thin air of an amok despair I'd been fucking with all morning. To prove this, rather than snort or shoot it, I tickle the DELete key on the computer keyboard a few times. Sure enough, a few one-byte holes appear in the brown powder exposing the gray case of the computer beneath. I hold down the key, and it "echoes" its function, right to left, bottom to top, just like a cursor on a screen, until I release it. When I do release it, the brown powder is gone.

I check the screen.

"I, alas, Mr. Windrow, will never again appreciate this magnificent instrument firsthand, as it were." Thimbelina lit another Gitane and blew a thick, blue smoke ring that spun and expanded in the air, encircling as it sank Tiny's massive penis and crashed into the monster's loins. Tiny sighed like a water buffalo. "But I assure you, Mr. Windrow, it's a thrill beyond heroin."

Aha. Oho. Oh no. What Have I Done? Still standing

over the keyboard, with a bunch of damp change in one hand and the multipurpose computer magazine in the other, I close the file WIND (the 9th Martin Windrow novel, gag me), and save it, exit the writing software (WordStar). The machine warm boots, as it should, but then this message pops up

```
(xsub active) ...
AØ>
```

What the fuck? XSUB is shorthand for the Extended Submit utility, copyright alla time by Digital Research and Gary Kildall, the brilliant author of CP/M, the operating system that runs my and tens of thousands of other people's computers. XSUB is a subset of SUBMIT—something my landlady understands better than I do—but on this machine is supposed to allow a long series or string of commands to happen, automatically, simply by calling the SUBMIT utility along with the name of the command routine. The first one I wrote, for example, after days of trial and error, I call KOPY.SUB. Simply entering SUBMIT KOPY at the keyboard formats a blank disc, places CP/M and three transient utilities on it, displays the new directory, and quits. Don't even need XSUB in there. But XSUB increases automation, if you want, allowing for example preconceived keyboard input to be entered from the program. The program runs things just as if there were an operator there, tapping in stuff from the keyboard; but, except to get things started, there needn't be an operator. Neat, huh?

You don't think so?

Well, how do you think I got nine Martin Windrow novels published?

Merit?

Thimbelina smiled distantly. "I don't think it's a question of merit, exactly, Mr. Windrow. I think it's more a question of . . . size. That, and lubrication."

Tiny grinned crookedly, cleared his throat, and spat on the palm of his hand.

Thimbelina blew concentric smoke rings at the night beyond the glittering, wet window pane.

But these SUBMIT routines can get very complicated, and moreover they are notorious for being erratic and unpredictable. What will run on one type of CP/M machine might not run on another, and what looks good in a routine you've been running since you wrote it, when slightly modified, might not work at all, or yield strange results.

After selling a couple of these Martin Windrow books, I realized that I could make an easy thing even easier by using a word processor to write them, instead of the old manual typewriter that Momma gave me when I was a prodigy. So I bought a computer. I won't mention the brand, as they might be touchy about having the words 'sodomy' or 'brainfuck' and 'Kaypro' in the same sentence, then run their own copyright protection SUBMIT SUE routine on me, in the megafucker mainframe they undoubtedly have down there in Solana Beach to keep an eye on such things.

The computer changed mah life, buddy. Oh, sure, it made writing easier, if only by eliminating the need for carbons, retyping entire drafts, even Xeroxing to a certain extent, and perfect touch-typing. In fact, it's not any exaggeration at all to postulate that the computer is the hottest thing to happen to writing since movable type; or ink, perhaps. But you already know that, doncha. Smart reader. But if you're so smart, how come you, if an average consumer, helplessly read 4.2 Martin Windrow mysteries a year? Huh? And this book, huh? Why don't you just put the motherfucker down and go to the beach? Or read Sidney Sheldon? There are a *lot* of books out there better than this one. In fact, I'd go so far as to say that, not only have I read a hell of a lot of books that have been better than the one you're holding right now, I've *written* any number of books better than this one. *So Long, Pockface* is a prime, I mean a prime example. The first Martin Windrow novel, *The Gourmet*, is another. *The Gourmet*, (recently reincarnated as *The Damned Don't Die*, Black Lizard Books, Berkeley, California, 94710, $4.95) was so good that, to this day, the memory of the fire in which it was forged, the heat by which it was conceived, the exhausting volume of sperm dripping from the underside of the desk at which I wrote it, to this very moment the memory of its creation haunts me. When, oh when, will I achieve such heights again?

". . . swipe haunts me to this day, Mr. Windrow, as it will you. Of course, the thrill of it will be somewhat mollified, in your mind, by the specter of the possibility of your having contracted AIDS from Tiny, as he rapes you. That's the risk you take with us, Mr. Windrow, that's it in a nutshell. Not only do you risk death, but a most grisly death: the most *grisly death." Thimbelina paused to consider the smoke rising from his cigarette. The rain ticked hesitantly against the window, the traffic hissed on the street below. Slippery, wet sounds came from Tiny's side of the room, as the leviathan slowly masturbated in the dark.*

Any writer worth his salt would confess to being unable to help himself, he has to write or go berserk, that's the choice, simple as that. Quality doesn't mean a thing. It's a nice thing to have, quality, kind of a dainty embellishment, but it's a tough thing to get away with and still eat. Off your writing, I mean. But a few good tools can only help the process, quality not withstanding. It's a carnal bozo that blames his tools, and it's another one that won't admit of a tool's utility. You laugh. After you've finished, go talk to some writers. In a group of five, you'll find two who would barricade themselves in their rooms and live off their own shit before they'd touch a computer keyboard, much less write on one. They'll give you all these terms, like logorrhea, techno-facism, rosy-throated finches, negative capability, and Keats didn't need one.

Well, you might tell them, take a look at the bright side. There's an outside chance a few months in front of a leaky cathode ray tube might give you a fine case of tuberculosis, like what took off John himself, or worse. Isn't that inspirational? And being sat in front of the thing at the time, you'll be in a position to do something about it, fingers nicely arched over the keyboard, wrists not touching, palms not resting on the chassis, like a consumptive concert pianist, propped to his last effort.

". . . inspirational, Mr. Windrow, by way of an early capitulation . . . to save yourself some pain—or pleasure—or, worse perhaps, the pain of admitting your own pleasure, no? You are, I believe, heterosexual, are you not Mr. Windrow? A confirmed hetero-sexual . . . ?"

It was only a year or two later that I really got into the operating system, how these machines work. At first it was intimidating. These machines are very powerful, do not doubt it. One doesn't simply start POKEing around. Well, some ones do. I did. Crashed the machine a lot, too. Inadvertently, at first; then, willfully. Software, hardware; new worlds and lots of them. If I'd been a kid when the small computers reached the homes of America, I'd be a different person today. As it is, things are bad enough . . . Marlene . . . Andrea . . . Mattie . . . Hadley . . . As it is, all my women friends, the women I sleep with, have soft 'a's in their names . . . A disconcerting bent . . . But Computer . . . There's a name without an 'a.' And she's my friend, it's true, and I have fallen asleep over her, like a drunk on a whore, and still she works on for me, still she willingly SUBMITs . . . .

That KOPY.SUB routine I mentioned earlier consummated my interest in submission. A year later, I wrote the one, the one that . . . But the heroin . . . That's a new one, that's getting a bit . . . potent . . . .

See, there's this trend in publishing. You've no doubt heard about it. Eccentricities to the contrary, more and more writers have turned to the computer to write. Simultaneously, leading the way in fact, more and more publishers have turned to computers to assist them in the act of publication. As a result, many writers now submit their manuscripts in disc form, especially writers who have a direct relationship going with a particular publisher, so they have all kinds of little things straight between them, things like disc format, operating systems, writing software, dot commands, etc. etc. Things that enable the writer to give the publisher a disc, all other things editorial having been taken care of, that is, capable of being converted directly from the writer's original into type, and thence into a book. A typeset book, with covers, art, blurbs, price and everything else added by whosoever does such things, by computer, along the way. It's a fantastic concept, and it's more than a concept. Modern quilldrivers do it every day, and so do their publishers.

Not only all that but, using modems and telecommunications, a writer far away or in a hurry or famous enough to get away with it, can *phone* his manuscripts to his publishers. To provide a well-known example, Arthur C. Clarke modems all his scripts, rewrites, changes and contracts back and forth from the outside world to and from fucking Sri Lanka, while sitting in front of his computer in a sarong, where the noted author maintains a small but serviceable paradise of electronic and natural synergy. This process of course involves even more software and hardware than the simple exchange of discs: equipment and programs that can dial the phone for you, at a certain time—any time, very late at night, for example, or on the weekend after New Year's Eve ... —access a certain area of the answering computer, deposit certain information there, retreat without leaving a trace . . . .

Does this give you any ideas?

It did me. I confess. Mea culpa, little disc drives, it gave me a whopper: BOOK.SUB.

I had this 'relationship' with a publisher. Like most such 'relationships,' this one hinged on a particular editor. She liked my writing, so she saw that this publisher, Crow Mignon Books, published my writing. Her name, by the way, was Matilde. Another 'a' name. Eastern European. Great guttural, salivaridden phone voice. Never actually saw her face to face. But it was Matilde who gave me my first good phone. It went something like this.

"Mr. Jameson?"
"Hello."
"Mr. Jas Jameson?"
"Hello hello."
"Well."
 Pause.
"Ahem."
"Very pleased to meet you, Mr. Jameson."

"And whom may I say I am pleasing?"

"Matilde, Matilde Michelov. I'm calling from Crow Mignon Books?"

"Crow—Oh! Oh yes! A publisher! Yes of course! I'm—I'm abjectly delighted to have, to be—meeting you?"

"Thank you, Mr. Jameson. I'm calling to suggest to you that we, I should say, I, I very much enjoyed *So Long, Pockface*, and I would like to do a presentation on it."

"Do a . . . ?"

"To the senior editor. But, of course, I must be certain that we wouldn't be wasting his time. First of all, I see by the postmark that it's been 2½ years since you mailed the manuscript to us. Has the book been published?"

"Are you kid—I mean, no, no, for some reason, I mean, by some incredible quirk of circumstance, it hasn't."

"No one else has been interested, then?"

"Well, that's not strictly true, Ms., Ms. . . . ?"

"Michelov. Matilde Michelov."

"Matilde. That's M, A, . . . ?"

"A, Sir, that's correct."

"That's a nice name."

"Thank you. Mother liked it, too. Now, you were saying . . . ?"

"I was saying, due to circumstances out of my control, the property you mentioned is still up for grabs."

"Well, Mr. Jameson . . ."

"Jas, Jas . . ."

"In a minute, Jas. As I was saying, Mr. Jameson, I'm in a position to offer you $1,500 for *So Long, Pockface*."

"Fifteen hundred dollars."

"That is correct."

"Ms. Michelov, this is a novel we're talking about here, not a crossword puzzle."

"Mr. Jameson, I certainly understand your concern, but you must take the broad view . . . ."

"I'm always taking the broad view, Ms. Michelov. We're talking about money and books here."

"Book, Mr. Jameson. A single book."

"Surely, Ma'am, surely you can understand, I've my life's blood in *So Long, Pockface*, I poured my soul into that book . . . ."

"We'll discuss the rewrite in a moment, Mr. Jameson, if and after we have an agreement. The figure under consideration was fifteen hundred dollars. American."

"Couldn't you manage two thousand, Ms. Michelov? I'm worried about my landlady. Not that she's said anything, but she seems so hungry of late, I'd love to be in a position to negotiate an increase in my rent . . . ."

"I'm sorry, Mr. Jameson. We have a budget here. We're perfectly willing to publish quality literature, in fact we're scouring the country for it, and what a marvelous fluke that we discovered your manuscript. Think of it! Hidden in our office these 2½ years!"

"Hidden?"

"With the telephone directories. We have a library of telephone directories in a special room here, the same one in which the janitor keeps all his stuff. Your manuscript was inexplicably tucked away with the California directories, where no one would ever find it."

"Why . . . why would no one ever find it there?"

"Oh, we never call California. Everyone's so weird out there, we're all afraid to use a California area code. It's so intimidating! And all those—those—"

"Queers?"

"Yes! Not that I'd ever use a term like that, but . . . ."

"Oh, they don't mind . . . ."

"I prefer 'gays' myself. It's much more descriptive."

"I don't know. 'Queer' suits some people better than others, and 'fag' works too, I guess, but if it's descriptive you're after, how about 'cocksuckers'?"

"Well, that term's not exactly exclusive, Mr. Jameson, if you know what I mean . . . ."

"No, I'm not sure I do, Ms. Michelov."

"I mean, you could call me a cocksucker, if you wanted to."

"I'd love to, Matilde."

"Would you let me, Mr. Jameson?"

"Oh, yes, Matilde. Absolutely."

"This darn phone . . ."

"It's hard . . ."

"Oh, is it?"

"And big . . ."

"Oh, I don't know if I can get my *lips*, my *mouth*, my *tongue*, around such a *big thing* . . ."

"Swollen, thick, stiff, hard, wet . . ."

"Oh, Mr. Jameson, I'm wet, too . . ."

"Put the phone down there, Matilde."

"Ohhhh . . ."

"That sounds pretty good."

"Mmmmm . . ."

"Does it feel—hello? Matilde?"

"Oh! Oh yes Mr. Jameson, I'm here. This is . . . I'm so . . . This is so unusual!"

"Are you alone, Ms. Michelov?"

"I have my own office, Mr. Jameson."

"Is the door closed?"

"Yes, I, I mean I think so! Oh! Oh, who cares!?"

"Certainly not I, Ms. Michelov, but I was wondering, do you have on a dress?"

"Not any more! I mean, it's up around my waist . . ."

"And stockings?"

"Yes, and heels. Do you like high heels, Mr. Jameson?"

"Yes, I do, Ms. Michelov."

"There's one on my typewriter, and one in the ashcan, Mr. Jameson. And I'm leaning back in my chair. What do you think of that?"

"It sounds rather abandoned, Ms. Michelov. Are you fingering yourself?"

"Oh! Yes, Mr. Jameson, I'm so wet."

"I'm reaching for the olive oil myself, Ms. Michelov. It's from the olive groves in the hills above Lucca, extra virgin olive oil, Ms. Michelov, the kind that smells so strongly, and I'm liberally slavering a handful all over my immense cock, with both hands, the telephone propped between my ear and my shoulder."

"Oh, Mr. Jameson, I've switched you to my speakerphone, so that I can massage my pussy and clitoris with one hand, I'm soaking wet, and reach around with my other hand, to massage the crack of my ass, getting it perfectly wet also, oh, I'm nearly spending sir, but I've still got time to insert two fingers of one hand into my wet asshole, and two fingers of my other hand into my cunt, abrading the while the hell out of my clit, which is— hsssss!—on fire!"

"Do it, Ms. Michelov, do it, while I twist and wring my swollen dick like a 14th-century religious candlemaker..."

"Oh! Mr. Jameson, I've scraped your manuscript off the top of my desk and onto the floor, and speared the title page with one of my black spike heels—!"

"Spike it again! Spike it again!"

"I'm lowering my ass over the speakerphone and massaging it wildly, no doubt you can hear the confused, erratic digital tones as my clitoris slips over the alphanumeric keypad, the prongs of the receiver hook enter my orifices, and—I'm coming! I'm coming! I'm coming!"

"I'll sign! I'll sign! I'll sign!"

"Oh! Mr. Jameson!"

"Oh! Ms. Michelov—Matilde—!"

"Jas!"

"Oh!"

"Oh!"

And so forth. One could hear the crash of furniture in New York, the jar of pencils, the typewriter, the telephone, the trash can, desk calendar, Rolodex, three or four wind-up toys and a plastic dinosaur, all of it, hit the floor before the phone went dead. Ten minutes pass, I'm having a beer and staring out the window. She calls back.

"About that rewrite . . ."

"What rewrite?"

"Just a few changes, Mr. Jameson. I'll make a note of them and send it along with the contract."

"Do I get paid for it?"

Silence. Then, "You're not serious."

"I suppose I'm not."

"Have you thought of investing in a computer, Mr. Jameson?"

"Yes."

"Well?"

"Can you deal with WordStar on a disc?"

"Wonderful!"

"Send me the contract."

"It's as good as in the mail."

Simple, wasn't it?

(xsub active) . . . .

THREE

I'm explaining this badly.

By the time Ms. Michelov wanted the revisions to *So Long, Pockface*, I was ready. I was ready long before she called, actually. It wasn't easy, being ready. But what was difficult was waiting for her to call. Waiting to pounce.

The research alone took sixteen weeks. Can you imagine? What kind of computer, for example, did Ms. Michelov have at her desk? An IBM XT? Oh, that's nice. An MS-DOS machine. Anybody out there realize the differences between CP/M and MS-DOS in 1985? Virtually incompatible. Major obstacle. But I'm cool. It's all theoretical anyway, at first. So, Ms. Michelov. And what sort of machine might you use on an author's disc formatted by another operating system? Oh, Mr. Jameson, we have translation software, very la-de-da. Really, Ms. Michelov. And an in-house whiz to keep track of it all. Of course, she confides, he doesn't know a thing about literature. Just computers. He different from *us*. A perennial problem with technical people. Probably saves him a lot of sleepless nights, I suggest. Oh, no, I don't think so, opines Ms. Michelov, he mostly works nights, we rarely see him around the office in the daytime. Pause. Excepting Fridays, of course. Fridays? Payday, you ninny. Ah, so. The eagle flies. Whaaaat? she whines. (I'm having second thoughts, sexually, is this what they call *triste*?) Old saying, pay it no mind, as it were, it's just that I, as a self-employed person, am unfamiliar with the mores of the American office worker. Vague me, baby. Oohhhhh, she vagues. (Third thoughts . . .) What's his name? Marvin. Marvin? Marvin Chompsky. You're. No I'm not kidding either. Chompsky. Anglicized somethingorother. Say, Matilde, today's Friday. May I have a word with Marvin . . . ? Et cetera.

Marvin is most helpful, as most computer people are. No matter what you tell them, information—the flow of nibbles, bits, and bytes—is never proprietary. Information is free. Old school, that. Things are changing. But Marvin is seventeen, making forty thousand a year working part-time, reading the electronic edition of the *Wall Street Journal* while he waits for the accounting department to figure out his latest check-writing scheme, issue him a check he can shoot to his broker, also seventeen years old. They're into it. Never trust anyone old enough to drink. I upload a pirated, upgraded, latemodel, superfast version of Zork to Marvin, and zap, Crow Mignon Books loses their computer whiz for a week. Not that I'm soliciting complicity, you understand. Maybe a little advance warning, before the crash. But so long as Zork is untamed in New York by one Marvin Chompsky, certain channels are open. Zork is a trojan horse, and I'm Greek. That's the way it is, you know. In spite of electronic wonders virtually beyond the imagination, I mean, *way* beyond what I'm trying to pull off with Crow Mignon Books, incredible as it may seem, certain kinds of game-consciousness are still regional to the West Coast. Yeah, yeah. I know all about MIT and the game of LIFE. But you can't play LIFE on a Kaypro, or even an XT.

But Marvin, he's got a mini-mainframe at his disposal there at Crow Mignon Books, he's the sysop for the whole outfit, and he's got a user area all to himself. Marvin the sysop has appropriated a sort of memory tithe, in addition to howeversomany eagles fly into his iguana wallet every Friday, by which larceny he has set himself up with this rather mammoth system to use according to his lights.

This is great, I like it in here. Memory is a warm, comfortable place. None of those insidious messages cropping up in ROM or on the screen, only Time to kill . . . .

I should mention, too, that, at the time in memory we are considering, Crow Mignon Books were in deep, deep financial difficulties. Chapter Eleven, bankruptcy loomed ineluctable. Only a miracle might have saved them although, consistent with their previous management policy, they wouldn't and didn't know a miracle when it hit them. Hit them it did, in the form of mammoth Martin Windrow receipts.

It seems that, although they had at least three lines of books that netted them millions in annual sales, the board of directors had spun off a massive amount of capital into, you guessed it, a computer company. Chaos reigned in the boardroom. Hell, CHAOS was the name of the computer company. Computers *Hold All OmniScience*, get it? Kind of a techno-religious outfit. One of their areas of expertise specialized in mortuary software. When Carry On, the holding corporation that owned Crow Mignon, first started to flirt with Chaos, the latter had projected annual sales, based on earnings reported through the second quarter, of $165 million. Six months after Carry On committed all of their cash and repossessables—all that is, with the exception of the $1,500 they intended to advance me against royalties derived from *So Long, Pockface*—CHAOS Technologies reported a remarkably lame $17 million in sales, canceled their dividend, boding worse prospects for the spring when, according to Silicon Valley market analysis, everyone is out fucking instead of buying computer products.

As a result, nobody, least of all the board of directors of Crow Mignon Books, all of whom were majority stockholders and officers of Carry On, Inc., having bled the publishing company dry, paid the least attention to the daily goings on of Crow Mignon. What with Marvin stoned on Zork in his exclusive User Area, 11235 (note the Fibonaccian spurt), I had the run of the system.

Not that I could run it. But with Marvin's absent-minded advice, I hacked it, and how. I modemed in there every night, late, about eleven o'clock, California time, which is two a.m. in New York. Marvin, having studied and sorted his rather intense stock portfolio and sleek routines for manipulating it five or six hours earlier, and having been disassembling or playing Zork ever since, was usually ready to exchange a few desultory words and call it a night, so far as my window into his world was concerned. He built me a little windowing routine by which, when I was in trouble or confused, I could open into his Zork screen and ask him a question. He would simply key out the answer and boot me off the screen if I were slow in leaving. The exchanges generally went like this.

```
Author 126, Hello
Hello. Password?
Felch
That's a good one. Enter.
Sir, the Klingons are aboard, Sir.
Good evening, Mr. Jameson. Are you writing tonight?
No. Touring. And yourself?
I'm stuck in level 22. The Princess won't yield me
her key.
Try plucking the lute.
I lost the plectrum somewhere between 19 and 21.
```

You can grow a plectrum-like thumbnail by remaining alive in level 14 for three iterations. Don't forget to specify which thumb.

Thank you. But, Mr. Jameson, will the Princess wait? Take the lute with you.

No more hints, please. By the way. What does Felch mean?

Forget it.

Thank you. I'm leaving to grow a thumbnail.

Marvin, wait.

Yes?

Who controls User 6?

Mr. Compton, the comptroller.

Oh. He wouldn't be using just any old password, would he.

Oh, no way. Have you a thesaurus?

No, but you do.

I <DEL> We do?

In Formatting and Editing, User 12.

Oh, yes. Ahem, I quite forgot. They do fool around, in there, I remember their clearing the compatibility of the purchase with SYSOP. A thesaurus and dictionaries take a heck of a lot of memory, Mr. Jameson, very inefficient. Things are much more interesting over in database.

SYSOP? Why didn't they just walk down the hall and ask you?

People carry germs, Mr. Jameson.

You're right, Marvin, I quite agree. BBS are a lot cleaner. Although, carrying germs is a lot of work. Someone has to do it, and it might as well be sapient creatures.

I'm sorry, Mr. Jameson, but changing levels garbaged your transmission. Ah. The jar of hormones?

I'll never tell.

I skipped it before.

Now all you have to do is fend off the spiders for three cycles.

With pleasure.

Have you seen the big one?

What big one?

Synonym for ... ?

WHAT BIG ONE

He only turns up on the third iteration, just when you think you've got that thumbnail grown. Comptroller ... Synonym for money?

Right the first time. What big o

Hey, thanks, Marv. User 12, fire thesaurus torpedo ...

Great Spock!

Big one, isn't he ... ?

It's a she!

If you found that out, you've already lasted longer than I did.

Monstrous, hairy ... Where's the heart—I left my sword on 23! All I've got it this fucking lute!!!

Bye

AAAHHHRGG!

*

\

Now, Marvin had this hack going, to which I was the willing guinea pig. Today, PRODOS, MS-DOS, PC-DOS, CP/M, MP/M, UNIX, PROLIX—they're all compatible on any big system, just like any user can program in Pascal, C, Forth—in short, speaking the language he or she speaks, and program away, the Translators look after the small stuff, the details. This of course enters into all sorts of philosophical domains, like if you are GOTOing in Basic, are you IF-THENing in Pascal, or whatever. Like, Total Syntax, if you care. I'm bullshitting here, apologies to the nine of you who know what I'm attempting to discuss, but all this aside, in the times I'm talking about, nobody had this translation thing together. Philosophy really does enter into the picture, as if two composers were trying to express the same idea in music, it really can and does get that deep, but Marvin, he had a compatibility thing going in this network of his.

Crow Mignon, when they thought about it—and they had, back when they had management who cared about books per se, and by extension the people who write them—had realized that by no means were they in a position to dictate the brand of computer their writers were to write on. That is a very personal decision, akin to telling you who you're going to sleep with tonight, or capitulating to predestination. One can handle only so much Calvinism. Ever tried to borrow a computer from a writer? He'll loan you his tractor, his wife, his fifth, his mule—never his computer. Right, let's don't forget the recidivist, who won't loan you his wax stylus, let alone his syntax, *because* it's different from what he thinks you *should* be handling. We're in a different class, here. Here, we're talking abject. After all, if we find a writer who can write (*the stuff*), why not cater to him to the extent that his computer can talk to our computer? Moreover, if it can, we save $thousands in typesetting costs, no?

And so it came to pass, more or less, that Marvin was engaged by Crow Mignon Books, Inc., to devise a means whereby all authors under serious consideration, given that they weren't of genius status (they weren't), and therefore had to knuckle under to the extent of owning a computer in the first place, if they wished to consider being published by CM Inc., might avail themselves of the marvelous labor-saving capacities of modern word-processing.

So far, so good. Like most hackers, Marvin was no dummy. Naïve, maybe. Inexperienced? Hard to believe, with Ms. Michelov perched just down the hall, but yes: Marvin was inexperienced. Not only that, he loved Zork.

The printing firm was a modem away. Another machine, set up to take particular control characters available in a .DOC file in user area Ø, readily downloadable to a disc file on my machine, dictated to the printer's computer the format, the files, the quantities ... Everything, in short, that anyone would need to know in order to print a complete book.

Cover art?

Hah.

The Thesaurus fires off its string.

```
User 12 <cr>
Password?
Money<cr>
Password?
Cash<cr>
Password?
Clams<cr>
Password?
Sequins<cr>
Password?
Lucre<cr>
A12>
```

In.

As you might surmise, this can take hours, days, and did. But eventually, after weeks of wandering around Crow

Mignon's in-house machine, with quite a few hints from Marvin, and not incidentally incurring a huge phone bill, until I discovered how to call the machine collect, after many nights, I say, of snooping this larger machine, I had discovered many things.

Pornography, for example. The Crow Mignon house computer had a huge selection of so-called 'boilerplate' passages of pornographic set-pieces, such as one might find in any 'Victorian' novel, by 'Anonymous.' Turns out Crow Mignon had published sixty such books, there was a list of them in an innocent-looking and obscure file labeled FLOWER.CAT., which in turn was a sub-category of a huge file called METNSPDS.DOC. Meat and spuds, doc. Get it? Out of curiosity, using a public domain utility running on my own machine, 3000 miles away, I queried the sixty FLR files concerning the frequency of occurrence of the PORNPA.TCH file labeled 3ON1PA.TCH, a pedestrian description of three men fucking a single woman. (The reciprocal, three women on a single man, was labeled 1ON3PA.TCH. Detect any sexism in the syntax? The masturbation routines were all in SCRATCHI.TCH.) The same passage, consisting of fourteen paragraphs, occurred in sixty books no less than 47 times. On a hunch, querying further, I discovered that 3ON1PA.TCH occurred more than once in fourteen of the files, or 'books,' by 'Anonymous'; and no less than three times in one of them, undoubtedly a mistake.

Naturally, I downloaded a couple of the ones I liked, erased two egregiously aprurient ones, replacing the latter with passages much improved in style, tone and lubricity. But I miss the point, which is that a certain printing house, Pre-Eminent Press Co., in Milwaukee, Wisconsin, printed these books for Crow Mignon, under the aegis of Amber Twilight Books, very cheaply, in large editions. Certain formatting codes presented themselves, which I downloaded into what later became a subroutine of BOOK. SUB. And not incidentally, Amber Twilight Books were at that time virtually supporting Crow Mignon Publishing; Crow Mignon had entered the field on the strength of a strong seller entitled *A Maid's Honour*, by Anonymous. I discovered Pre-Eminent's telephone number and had the Crow machine call it. A computer answered. And it was menu driven!

```
Hello. Your Account No. Please?
```

This would take awhile. I hung up and subsequently found the Amber Twilight I.D. number over in accounting. Returning and entering it, I found my screen filled with courtesy.

```
Checking............
Thank you, Amber Twilight.
Would you like to
Speak to Accounting?      (1)
Speak to Sales?           (2)
Speak to Production?      (3)
Order Job?                (4)
Print Job?                (5)
Ship?                     (6)
Quit?                     (7)
Enter Selection:          _
```

Miraculous. I now had cachet with Pre-Eminent Press, a huge printing concern, whose trifecta in life was to produce massive amounts of cheap paperback books, ship them to distributors all over the world, and bill somebody for their trouble. After a few weeks of hacking all over the East Coast and Midwest, I had lined up accounts with distributors as well, and was in business with every writer's dream: a publisher, printer, and distribution network that would disseminate my books *at my will* to bus stations, cigar stores, airports, and newsstands all over North America and 18 English speaking countries, within two months of completion and 'acceptance' of the manuscript. Soon I was up every night, hacking away in the Crow Mignon computer. I downloaded their old royalty schemes and uploaded new ones, slightly more favorable to not only myself but to all their other authors as well. I downloaded their standard blank contracts, rewrote and uploaded them, keeping a copy on disc to print out, sign, and mail to Crow Mignon's Legal Department as additional agreements were called for. I uploaded *Squeam with a Skew*, a new Martin Windrow novel, formatted according to their specifications, into a slot only six books behind *So Long, Pockface* in the production schedule. Carefully, I monitored the latter's progress through the system. *So Long, Pockface* had been in the works for over a year and was nearly ready for publication. Each night I logged on and snooped the files to see what had happened to *Pockface* that day, and kept notes. I even fabricated electronic editorial correspondence between myself and Ms. Michelov on the subject of *Squeam*, consistent with the few non-prurient words we'd exchanged over slight revisions designed to get the libel out of *Pockface*. Every writer's dream.

Of course, this entire operation took up days, nights, and weeks. Within six months I had *So Long, Pockface* and *Squeam with a Skew* out of production and into the bookstores, with *Cable Car to Hell* and *This World Leaks Blood* creeping up the assembly line. The Michigan printers suddenly found themselves producing reams of promotional material on an unprecedented scale, for an ad campaign hyping Martin Windrow books. Sales were up, returns were down. Shipping orders began to increase, too. 'Dumps', not the hexadecimal kind, but cardboard matrices gaudily displaying a 4×8 array of the latest Martin Windrow novel, suitable for an endcap or display near the cash register or anyplace else conspicuous, began to appear in your finer chain bookstores. But things were so chaotic at Crow Mignon that I had to run almost the entire business by myself. To save money, the staff had been halved. Marvin was down to a couple of days a week, and Ms. Michelov's job, she told me, hung by a thread. I had to do everything. Ms. Michelov, although achieving some credibility behind the sales of the Windrow books, could not expect a few pulp detective thrillers to save the entire company. Consequently, she became increasingly involved with ghostwriting a cookbook authored by a famous football player, to the executive mind then holding sway a surefire cash cow. I was left with the entire operation and management of the Amber Twilight Windrow series. Increasingly, I could not cope with these business matters, and still be expected to write the damn things. Not to mention to deal with Marlene. Not to mention to do nothing, daydream, relax, invest, drink a beer . . . . Not to mention to keep ahead of Marvin in Zork. Not to mention I fell behind in my reading, in particular of the ongoing marvelous pornographic adventures of the beautiful and sluttish Italian vampire, Sukia, to which series I maintain a subscription. Creditors dunning Crow Mignon began to turn up in windows on my Zork screens, deflected there by a little routine Marvin had devised to keep them off his own back.

A pre-ulcerous condition loomed.

Automation became imminent.

FOUR

Returning phone calls is a pain in the ass, you know that. But try returning a bunch of calls to a computer. Christ, you can't even flirt with it. Well. That's not strictly true, actually. Silicon is reasonably lubricious, I suppose, if you're feeling 'that way'—'bloody rutty', as Anonymous would say. Brushing the palm of your hand over a field of transistor chips and dip switches, feeling the bits slip in, out, on, off ... Digging the absolute silence of the machine's response, wondering if you're getting it off, doing the right thing, lasting long enough ... Remembering how you did this thing before, and it'd be a shame to break off and check the records *now*, just when the machine's about to write and tell its mother how perfect everything is ... And then there're the perennial matters of taste and elegance, precisely the twin nemeses one generally locks oneself in the house to get away from ... The hours of imperfection limping from ashcan to ashcan in the mental streets, scavenging sustenance ... And suddenly, in a wire waste receptacle ... Taste and Elegance, two obese, short geriatrics in matching pineapple shirts, orange and yellow, blue ... find The Sunday *New York Times*! Well read, already smelling of cigars and ink and cinders and urine, the want ads wrapped around a load of dog shit, discarded but semi-intact ... harbinger of cultural awareness, the City, the Nation, the World, municipal trash ... And there they stand, Taste and Elegance, an old man and an old woman in identical Hawaiian shirts and thong sandals, their heads shaved for lice, ripping fewer and fewer pages of the Times out of each other's swollen fingers . . . I want Arts & Leisure, I want the City, I want Fashion, Travel, Real Estate . . . more and more pages fluttering torn to the ground, the two toothless mouths gumming obscenities, too arthritic to settle for Sports, toe to toe, four hands on the Times . . . Pigeons at their feet . . . People cross the street to avoid them . . . .

Taste and Elegance. These SUBMIT routines are funny. So are detective novels. But insofar as they have to survive, there're a lot like the phone, they don't need one another; they just need us.

```
Q<del>
; we need them.
SAVE
(xsub active) . . .
```

. . . overweight polysexual criminal out there in the hall just waiting to pounce on your child/mother/daughter/husband/loved one/self and give them a taste of the old badinage, scratch that, syphilitic appendage, it was Oscar Wilde, wasn't it, who'd rather give a taste of the old syphilitic badinage . . . wasn't it? But appendage will do, go to thesaurus, let's make badinage the code word for this file, remind me not to forget it I'd hate to lose this chapter after all I've been through to get to it, I told you to screen all my calls *except* for Ms. Michelov, let her through, use the loop routine BIZWIZ, handle that stuff for god's sakes, can't you see I'm trying to write? How do I expect myself to continue to be a productive arm of this concern if I'm constantly attending to these ridiculous business details? What's a publishing routine for, anyway? Take the book, publish it, send me the checks. That's it. Wait.

A clipping service. Invent the routine CLIP.SUB. Another week of sleepless nights.

And don't forget to copy me every review, goddammit.

Wait a minute here, dear reader. Let's get something straight. I'm talking to myself, not to the machine. You weren't seriously thinking that I was going to sit here and try to tell you this goddamn machine took over my life, were you? That it 'took on this mysterious life of its own?' 'The machine anticipated my every thought—nay, my every afterthought . . .' 'Even after its sluttish advances I continued to resist it, until, late one night . . . I'd been slaving over the CON:, writing at white heat. Never before had the lubricities spewed with such facility, the gore gushed, the rancor so articulate, the word count so tumescent . . . Surely, my subconscious was thinking, as I typed furiously, here smoked a career carried over the Alps by Hannibal . . . When, suddenly, I noticed the most marvelous, the most mysterious, the most frightening thing . . . The screen was actually *anticipating* my thoughts, even as I struggled to express them! Be it ever so humbly . . . Were I to type so fast, I'd be a marvelous secretary! But we continued unrelenting. Yes, we: the machine and I! Pages, chapters, Parts One and Two and Three virtually spewed forth! It's a Trilogy! The magic was exhilarating, intoxicating! Marvelous vistas of prose opened up and unrolled before my eyes at such consummate velocity I could *hardly read them*! The coprophilia of the ages regurgitated onto the CRT:, entered the disc, burst the bounds of the limited memory of the print spooler, sloughed pages (paginated, oh! so fortunately) to and fro on the floors, the furniture, the shelves of my study. Ankle, knee, balls deep! A whole book in a single night!

'And as dawn's polluted fingers caressed the diseased cock of the Transamerica Pyramid, I lay exhausted: limp and hysterical, draped across my machine, with what horror, yet with what unspeakable fascination, did I watch the following message scroll up the big green screen . . .

```
Poor Mr. Jameson.
You've worked very hard.
You must be very tired.
Would you like a back-rub, before we resume our
labors . . . ?'
```

Nope. None of that obtained nor obtains. Phooey. No sentient mess of tentacled bread boards and feelie-feelie chips with sixteen ruby light-emitting diode eyes was taking over my life, like some kind of hideous sapient mold in your refrigerator, that one night gets out and digests the cat. We're not transubstantiating any such shit to New York for Immediate Release. Maybe such things happen, maybe not. There are rumours of prescience, clairvoyance, dark forces . . . I'm not denying that I personally, for one, know someone, who knows someone, who has a sister who saw the 22 Fillmore crash into the power station, killing everyone aboard, just after it passed her as she was going through the trash looking for a transfer, and, had she immediately discovered one, would have jumped on the bus without giving it a thought. But, instead, *something*, no one could say *what*, exactly, made her space out on some kind of guru circular she found in there, the former science-fiction author movie stars endorse, and, reading it top to bottom, front to back, never found a transfer in time, and *missed the bus*. Lived to tell the story. Made the *Inquirer*. Clairvoyance? Or Divine Providence? Aeyup . . . . Nope, that's not what I'm trying to lay on you, here, gentle consumer. I'm not trying to tell you that somehow, somewhere, there was a computer up there (points) looking out for the welfare of the sister of the friend of my friend (smiles). In point of fact, I believe her welfare was canceled very soon after the time of this accident. (Smile off.) But, as you might imagine, at that point in time they were grateful enough just to be alive.

Nope. As you might expect, nothing's ever that simple around Marlene's house, nothing. Ever. And it's not just that she gets horny reading Humour in Uniform.

I wrote the SUBMIT routine, and called it BOOK.SUB. No big deal. Just sixteen weeks, hacking mainly at night. During the day I wrote *Through a Mandible, Delicately*, at that time the sixth or seventh Martin Windrow novel, already I was losing track. This powerful medicine always leaves trenchant fumes drifting through the head . . . Subroutine to keep track of them all . . . Of course you must realize that I've written several subroutines to keep track of them all, having either forgotten the names of the previous ones or where I stored them, or lost the subroutine that keeps track of the subroutines that keep track of the Martin Windrow novels, alphabetically, chronologically, financially, I had to go to a hard disk, etc. etc. Do you know the Shelley?

> Lift not the painted veil which those who live
> Call Life: though unreal shapes be pictured there,
> And it but mimic all we would believe
> With colours idly spread,—behind, lurk Fear
> And Hope, twin Destinies; who ever weave
> Their shadows, o'er the chasm, sightless and drear . . .

Through a Mandible, Delicately was my Hope, and assembly language my Fear. These danced—lascivious, pansexual, grotesque—insane harpsichordy quadrilles with Taste and Eloquence. Want to know a little routine that asks you your name?

```
;   File:   HELLO.ASM
;
    ORG 0100H
;
    MVI C,9    ;Ask for name
    LXI D,ASK
    CALL 5
;
    MVI C,10   ;Read the name
    LXI D,BUF
    CALL 5
;
;   Put a space between "Hi," and the person's name.
;
    LXI H,BUF
    MVI M,20H   ;ASCII space, or blank
    INX H
    MOV E,M   ;Get number of characters in answer
    MVI M,20H
    MVI D,0
    INX H
    DAD D
    MVI M,'!'
    INX H
    MVI M,'$'
;
    MVI C,9    ;Say 'Hi,'
    LXI D,ANS
    CALL 5
;
    JMP 0000   ;Return to CCP
;
    ASK:  DB 'What is your name? $'
    ANS:  DB 0DH,0AH,'Hi,
```

```
'BUF:  DB 65   ;Buffer size is 65 characters
```

Notice the mnemonic DAD D. A few weeks of this stuff, and you're ready to holler for your UNCLE D, if only to quote you the Shelley.

But the SUBMIT routine is different. This is an operating system transient command. You can get SUBMIT to run routines like HELLO (after they've been assembled and loaded), and you can get XSUB to plug in appropriate console input. And brother, it's simple. All you really gotta do is blow off a lot of sleep and read a bunch of books. Then you take a stiff drink and a deep breath. Now hold it. Then you expel the trapped air suddenly onto the CRT screen, fogging it over. In a burst of nervous tension you kick back your chair, get up and pace around your oak and formica, ergonomically hip work station (optional extra), or your old pool table, your kitchen table, whatever. Then, finally, when you've worked up enough nerve, you create the file HELLO.SUB.

```
XSUB
HELLO
Fame and Fortune
```

This is after you've assembled, debugged, and loaded HELLO.ASM, above, of course, which process, while taking a little longer maybe than HELLO.SUB, has yielded the new transient program HELLO.COM. If you were to merely call HELLO at your prompt, you get a screen that looks like this.

```
A0>HELLO
What is your name?
```

You, flattered that the machine would ask, reply, from the console,

```
Fame and Fortune<cr>
```

And the machine immediately responds.

```
Hi, Fame and Fortune!
```

Much to your astonishment, or astoneagement, as Jas Joyce would say. Now, this is all well and good, a nice lesson in 8080/Z80 assembly language, out of date these 10 years. But, say you were sick of typing cute replies to dumb questions from your computer today, but, for some reason, you would really like to see a cute if predictable reply to a dumb question from your computer with minimum effort. If you merely embed HELLO.COM in a SUBMIT file, then called it thusly,

```
A0>SUBMIT HELLO<cr>
```

you would see HELLO's question on your screen

```
What is your name?
```

but you would still have to type the reply,

```
Fame and Fortune
```

forcing the machine to salute obsequiously:

```
Hi, Fame and Fortune!
Warm Boot
A0>
```

XSUB, however, allows the user to preselect keyboard input, in this case 'Fame and Fortune', so that if you want to set things going and just watch, so-called 'green-screen voyeurism', a common malady among graphics freaks, just type

```
AØ>SUBMIT HELLO
```

which goes looking for HELLO.SUB, and finding it, shows you

```
Warm Boot
AØ>XSUB
AØ>HELLO
What is your name?
Fame and Fortune
Hi, Fame and Fortune!
(xsub active) ...
Warm Boot
AØ>
```

in its entirety, no further input needed. Moreover, short of unplugging the machine, it can be difficult to interrupt or interdict XSUB once it's been set going. Notice the parenthetic reminder concerning who's in charge. Is it insidious yet?

If there were a second command, or further keyboard input applicable to the HELLO.COM routine, the SUBMIT program, after printing the parenthetic reminder, would run until all had been completed. After each completed program, the prompt (xsub active) or (xsub still active) comes up on the screen. There are many file functions, file manipulations and other matters that need never send information to the screen. And, of course, if whatever it is you're doing precludes any interest you have in seeing its various functions output to the screen, you can just rewrite the BIOS calls accordingly, so that when programs are running, the operator, or the person watching the screen, need never be the wiser. This is particularly true for a large machine, whose video terminals wouldn't want to get completely tied up by such a simple little thing as, say, publishing a book. Like the machine at Crow Mignon.

Finally, take a look at this.

```
:100100000E09112D01CD05000E0A114601CD050085
:10011000214601362023 5E362016002319362 1237E
:100120003624 0E09114101CD0500C3000057686156
:10013000742069732 0796F7572206E616D653F2040
:07014000240D0A48692C415F
:0000000000
```

That's the entire HELLO.ASM routine assembled into hexadecimal format, one step closer to what the computer actually reads when you implement the command HELLO. Tiny, isn't it? It's an ant on the elephant of memory. You could hide something that size almost anywhere, let alone in the vast memory of a big machine; like, say, in the machine at Crow Mignon Books . . . .

And you know what it comes down to? A modest series of intermittent beeps and whistles, a little white noise, in the audio background of a little session with Ms. Michelov. That's all. Then the same between Crow Mignon's computer and Pre-Eminent's, a little more tweeting between the latter and various distributors, and between those and the retailers . . . Next thing you know the book's been remaindered . . . Little chapters sneaking along the phone lines, one computer to another . . .

nobody ever had the slimmest idea . . . It sounded like the distant calls of a sheepherder, enthusiastically encouraging his flock to get home before dark . . . Yes, almost bucolic . . . In the thick crepuscular light you can hear the bells on the rams, far down the arroyo, and smell the piquance of burning mesquite and scalded coffee, and there goes a straggle of ravens, chuckling themselves home to roost, they own a chain of bookstores . . . .

Is it insidious yet?

FIVE

I couldn't take it any more and left the house. Marlene provocatively straddled the long chromium wand of her vacuum cleaner as I squeezed past her on the narrow landing. She wore a summery lavender house dress with large yellow bougainvilleas on it, its loose bodice caught at the waist between her breasts and hips by a broad elastic woven into the material, and suspended from her shoulders by a couple of slim ribbons that left most of her back exposed. "Excuse me," I said, over the roar of the vacuum cleaner. She looked at me dreamily and placed her lips very close to my ear, pressing the vibrating hose between us. "What," she breathed into my ear, completely in symphony with the roar, "I can't hear you . . ." Her hands slid down my shoulders to my hips. She wore no shoes, certainly she wouldn't wear anything under the lavender and yellow dress. Even as my resolve began to disintegrate I muttered something to the effect that I must take the air. Marlene smiled and turned her back on me. As she leaned into her work her buttocks brushed my pelvis. I was pressed between these and the wall as she moved the vacuum hose from side to side over the ancient hall carpet. My hand involuntarily strayed up the thin Dacron over the vertebrae of her spine, and onto the naked field beyond. My fingers plowed into the luxuriant tangle of hair at the nape of her neck, her hair was reddish blonde, but a tail of pure gold lay hidden there, I knew, beneath the strawberry curls and just above the hollow at the base of her neck, it flashed at me as I combed her hair with my fingers. She turned her head from side to side, against my palm. Much woman, Marlene O'Shaughnesy, this marvelous landlady, I thought to myself, but I must take the air, and I pushed her gently forward, stepped toward the stairs, and released her. She rocked gently backwards against the wainscot and bounced back into her work, humming "The Long and Winding Road."

On the street the sun shone brightly, and a cool breeze with a tang of salt on it blew briskly from the west. Marlene's house was an immaculate Victorian facing the south side of Alta Plaza Park, a block off Fillmore Street, in a neighborhood full of immaculate Victorians so expensive as to virtually assure that each contained a two-income executive couple or a bordello of international reputation. As I approached the steps that rose from the sidewalk north into the park, a lemon yellow two-seat Mercedes convertible pulled into a driveway across from me, and a woman in a uniform dating from the reign of Victoria herself, rather like a maid's costume, a black satin camisole, trimmed with scarlet piping, black stockings, loosely wrapped withal by a white fur stole, exited the vehicle, leaving the top down and slamming the door. She precisely crushed a cigarette beneath the sole of her ebony high heel pump, carefully sectioned and draped the length of her impeccably groomed platinum blonde hair, so that three-fourths of it cascaded over her shoulders down to the middle of her back, the other one fourth over her ample bosom beneath the stole, and tripped purposefully up the steps of a lovely house, also facing the park, not four doors down from Marlene's, and let herself in with her own key.

Pausing at the top of the concrete steps, fifty yards up the hill and into the park, I turned and scanned the automobiles parked along the block I call home. Behind me, children squealed with delight as their maids, *au pairs*, tutors, and rarely a mother or two pushed them in chain swings with canvas seats. The A-frame swing-sets, rusty from years in the salt air, squeaked loudly in a half-acre sandbox in the middle of the fenced-off kiddie park, beneath a tall grove of eucalyptuses that rattled and swayed in the afternoon westerly.

After awhile I spotted him, asleep in a four year old Plymouth parked across the street a few doors down from the house with the Mercedes in its driveway. All the signs were there. Sections of the Chronicle, the green sports page well-read and on top, piled on the dashboard, along with a digital clock, sandwich wrappers and several white styrofoam cups—deli food and coffee. The car was a mess inside, but not too dirty outside, according to the recent rains and the caliber of the neighborhood. But parking places were very difficult to find here, undoubtedly the vanguard of the detail had spent most of their shift lurking around waiting for someone to vacate a space, and not just any space. So, once they'd scored a good one, they would rotate shifts but not cars, let alone parking places. At this point, any number of cops had sat in that old Plymouth, watching their quarry down the street. By now, the inside of the car would smell like a bus station bathroom. The ashtray would be filled to overflowing with butts and gumwrappers. Coffee would have been spilled on the floors and seatcovers. The odors of mustard, chilidogs, onions, farts, cigars and cigarettes, newsprint, fried electronics would have mixed with the disgusting native odor of Plymouth upholstery to the extent that only a man who had been in there already for seven or eight hours could stand it, by virtue of being used to it. And there he was, behind the wheel, Martin Windrow

himself. Unshaven, tie knot loosened, collar unbut-
toned, head thrown back against the seat, sound asleep.
His coat was thrown open, and you could see the ugly
checkered grip of his pistol sticking out from under his
arm against the white of his shirt. Any kid with time on
his hands might have reached in the open window and
blown out the guy's brains with his own gun. His snoring
mouth looked like the final hole in the final game of the
U.S. Open. It's a good thing for him there are no flies in
California. Asleep on the job,

*... and who can blame him. Only a novice or a dedicated man
can stand to stay awake on a boring and repetitive stakeout.
It's very cozy in a Plymouth in the sun on the lee side of the
park, and a man gets tired of keeping a close eye on something
he'd either rather fuck or try not to think about ...*

Actually, Windrow drives a Toyota. Or did, until it was
destroyed in an ass-kicking car chase in *Ulysses's Dog*.
Then he switched to a red '64 Ford Fairlane V-8, a classic.

But a disconcerting thought came to me as I stood
there in the breeze, and a sudden chill racked my frame.
The hookers had been in the neighborhood for a long
time. Why had they not been busted before? Maybe they
had. Perhaps I'd not heard about it. They were good neighbors, too. They belonged to the neighborhood association,
which had gotten some trees planted along the sidewalks
in front of our houses, and successfully fought against a
liquor license being issued to a man who wanted to open
a fern bar down on the corner. The hookers gave lots
of quality candy to the local kids on Halloween, nary a
razor-bladed bonbon or PCP-laced sucker in the lot. They
caroled the eight blocks forming the square around the
park every Christmas with members of the Episcopal

choir, but otherwise never made too much noise or had to have the cops come tell them to turn down their stereo. They had tastefully if gaily painted their house just a couple of years ago, gave a fifth of cognac to the mailman and a case of beer to the garbagemen every New Year. They had even caught a cat burglar breaking into the house next door to them. The hookers were, by anyone's standard, decent neighbors. One might go so far as to speculate that the neighborhood would rise up in arms, were the girls to get busted, but one also suspects the hypocrisy of one's neighbors. Besides, hookers break the law.

And the thought that chilled me, as I stood there in the wind, was: of course, they're not the only ones around here breaking the law. Are they. Nope.

At that precise moment, the cop in the Plymouth, whom I no longer was sure was in the vice squad, stirred in his sleep. A long arm stretched out of the window on the driver's side, shooting its cuff, bent double, and presented the wrist with the watch back into the window for the inspection of the awakened sleeper. And I jumped a foot, a queer little hop, which reversed my direction and launched me into the walk I'd intended from the beginning, which rapidly took me through the eucalyptus grove teeming with squealing children, and its benches lined with watchful women. It seemed to me then that the penalties pertaining to computer fraud were much stiffer than the ones applied to prostitution. And rightly so, I mused, as I circled past the hedges beyond which soft, periodic thwops betrayed the presence of tennis courts. Though not as noble an enterprise, computer crime is a much loftier offense to the public good than mere prostitution. And incredibly enough, this was the first time, since the very beginning of my endeavors, that the potential illegality of BOOK.SUB had so much as crossed my mind. So involved had I become in the theory of its enactment, the creation of the books necessary to test and employ it, the intricacies of the routine itself, the telephone networks interdicted by it, the computer knowledge I had necessarily gained to implement it, that, no one will ever believe you Jas, but so thoroughly had my mind taken up the project that the specter of prison as a reward only now presented itself.

A helicopter abruptly exploded over the rooftops of the houses to the east of the park, banked sharply not 500 feet overhead, and blasted south toward the Western Addition. Though such an intrusion is not uncommon in any city, I was momentarily terrified. Hardly anyone else strolling in park paid it any notice. But as my fear subsided, the question remained. Who, exactly, were those policemen in my neighborhood watching? Me? Or someone else? Were they vice or were they bunko?

Phrasing the question that way had a certain pleasing ring to it and I repeated it to myself as I continued to walk, are they vice or are they bunko, are they vice or are they bunko . . . And then I asked myself, what the fuck is bunko? We all know what vice is, we appreciate many forms of vice, but bunko, bunko, what is this bunko, and, is BOOK.SUB bunko?

"Bunko, you slime," Martin Windrow intoned evenly, "is to con, to swindle. It's what scum like you do to little old ladies with pension funds who don't know any better than to sign them over to the first scumbag that walks in the door and asks for it. It's like fraud, only a lesser crime, maybe involving lesser funds, and, since it's such an innocuous thing to be doing with your time, that scumbags like you like to jazz it up by raping, bludgeoning, and slicing into the bargain, so as to get a little press, so you know by reading your name in the newspaper you're alive, on account of the fact that you're dead inside. Putrifacted. Gone. Just a bag of scum with a sap in his pocket and a couple of big ideas he got when his father locked him in a closet in a hotel room in 1962. You carry these ideas around in that receptacle tip up on top there you call a head. But you don't want to be engaging on any of these one or two ideas with anybody that might offer a difference of opinion you might not be able to handle. So you do a couple of dry runs on little old ladies, ideally in wheelchairs and blind, that you can say to yourself are practically dead anyway, and if they can't take the little punishment you have to dish out to them to make them cough up the mortgage or their savings passbook or a sock stuffed with 252 dollars in ones and fives and loose change, why then they deserve to die, if they can't take a little taste of the sap . . . ." Windrow looked from the one hoodlum to the other, lurking in the shadows outside the yellow cone thrown by the dirty lamp on the bedstead. "But those little old victims are nowhere near as dead as you guys, nowhere near it. They got kids and grandkids, they had husbands and lovers, mothers and fathers, that cared for them and that they took care of and that took care of them. They saw World War II, they heard Martin Luther King speak, they gave to the United Way and to the Salvation Army, they saved somebody's kid from drowning in a frozen lake. And when they got old, and alone, when everybody was dead or gone off raising their own kids or too busy or too crazy and fucking up and forgetting who they are and where they come from, and they leave their old ones alone a little too much for whatever reason, but alone just long enough for buzzards like you to find them, to torture them and strip them and kill them and even rape them. That's when . . . That's when . . ." A zebra of yellow light streaked across Windrow's vision and his voice failed him, he nearly lost consciousness again. His head lolled onto his shoulder and he drooled on himself. The light from the lamp hurt his eyes. ˙

"Yeah?" said a shadow to his right. "Yeah, Windrow? Keep going, Windrow, this is interesting."

"Yeah," Windrow whispered, "yeah. That's when a little felony, a big bunko, becomes . . . becomes . . ."

"Becomes . . . ?" the other voice coaxed.

". . . Becomes interesting, becomes capital crime, murder, and if you get caught, when you get caught . . . ."

The other man laughed quietly. "When I get caught."

"You burn."

"I burn."

"B . . . b . . ." Windrow couldn't talk any more.

The shadow approached him. "Well that's fine, Windrow. That's just fine. You through now? You got anything else to tell me about my career?"

"F . . . f . . . fuck . . . y-y . . ."

"I thought so," said the voice, and the blackjack came down on Windrow's mind.

There's a porn theater on Chestnut St. where I like to go to think. It's a nice joint, as such joints go, maybe too nice, depends on your taste, but by that I mean there's nobody in the place offering to blow you in the dark, distracting you from your train of thought long enough to tell them yes or no, thank you. It's the kind of place straight couples go in and out of holding hands. Some of them are shy, some smiling, some furtive; they're cute to watch. And the films are mindless enough, so they don't distract you, either. Once in awhile you see something that's very funny, or very stupid, and very occasionally, rarely, something that's horny. But those are the exceptions. Usually the sounds are the same, the visuals are the same, the people are the same. Production values have improved over the years, it's true. These days you see fewer pimples on the untanned body parts, competent follow-focus, and less of the really disgusting mistakes people can make while they're trying to do outrageous sexual stunts in front of a camera. But by and large there's nothing to distract you, you can just sit there and think, with popcorn if you want, the wall of mindlessness flickering up there like a big hearth in a dark library, so that, even if you were paying attention the absurdity of it all would dawn on you eventually. I mean, in the close-ups the dicks are fifteen feet tall, and the vaginas are automobile-sized portals to other worlds . . . . Well maybe there's something to consider in there . . . . But like a beach or a church it's a good place to think . . . .

This day was no different than any other. There are little incongruities I like about the location. Chestnut St. is a 'nice' neighborhood. There's a flower shop down the street, an old Italian market, a couple of banks, a fair newsstand full of magazines and newspapers with cigars and of course Amber Twilight books mixed in with the pornography in the back. There are several well-known restaurants and fern-type bars, another, straight, movie theater, liquor stores, respectable town houses and apartment buildings. Amongst it all is this pornographic theater. Usually such things keep to their own neighborhoods, in San Francisco these would be the Tenderloin and North Beach, maybe the Financial District, period. Nowhere else, particularly an upstanding neighborhood featuring mothers strolling their babies, merchants sweeping their sidewalks, a store across the street specializing in jogging *equipage*. But the anomaly persists. Pay six bucks at the turnstile. Get some popcorn, if you like, above a glass countertop full of fleshly videotapes, condoms, and small tubes of ruby lubricants. Pass through a spanking clean lobby, paved in no-longer-obtainable linoleum. Enter through swinging brushed stainless-steel doors with portholes in them. Try not to trip over masturbators as you find a relatively isolated corner in the dark to relax in, an area—volume, really—whose neutrality will at first seep into your brain and cool it off, filling it with nothingness, before, rested, the mind begins to push its boundaries outward again, and fill not only your head but a territory several seats in diameter with its thrash and conflict and ideas, like the shavings and dust piled up behind a radial arm saw. There're never too many people in the place, especially in the middle of a sunny afternoon, when it's so bright outside that it takes a customer's eyes a full five minutes to adjust to the total darkness of the theater. So you lean against the high rail between the entrance and the seats, eating popcorn, studying the seating arrangements by the light bouncing off the creamy thighs up on the screen. When you find an area without too many heads slouched down in the seats, or none, you then figure a way to get to it without having to step over another patron, so as not to interrupt any jerking off, or disturb his or her—a lot of women come with their men to this theater, the films are rigidly heterosexual—private whatever. Or, hell, for all I know, everybody in the place is in there mainly to think, to escape into a vacuum from everything else, like me. After all, anybody in San Francisco who wants real pornography can settle for a lot more than just a movie.

But escape, as we all know, is a relative thing, if possible at all. I found a seat. I had no popcorn. I just sat there. The film apparently had attained some peak of interest, for it was tangibly quiet in the theater. A lot of oohhs and ahhs were coming out of the sound system. These effects were intended to convey intimacy. But they were loud, and thereby ridiculous. The scene of a woman sucking off a man was basically a quiet one, punctuated only by the kind of sounds you might ordinarily expect from a hushed party of spelunkers feeling its way through a damp cavern. Someone loudly cleared his throat in the balcony, but it was badly synchronized with the opening of a zipper, which was plainly audible. The effect was so theatrical, as if deliberate, that someone laughed on the other side of the theater.

This business of the Moral Imperative annoys me. In my line of work, detective novels, and in thrillers in general, while the clichés are bad enough, one is constantly grappling with the Moral Imperative. Which is, the bad guy gets his comeuppance in the end, period. Black and white, bad and good, plain as day the justice is meted. One cannot simply allow the criminal to escape unscathed by the vehemence of his own crimes. Either his conscience drives him mad, or the sheriff drives him to jail. Frequently, he's betrayed and done in by the depravity of his *milieu*. This is irony. Check out any Jim Thompson novel.

The variations on this scheme are endless as they are boring. Once in awhile one of my colleagues comes up with a new wrinkle, but it's usually as annoying as it is unoriginal. The net result remains the same. One way or another, by hook or by crook, the bad guy gets his dessert in the end. The Moral Imperative must prevail.

No one is prejudiced much, either, about how this comes about. Since Poe let the cat out of the bag we have seen criminals 'sent over' by Chinese aristocrats, corpulent aristocrats, cocaine addicts, faggots, little old ladies, Navajo Indians, cowboys, gourmets, guys with scars on their faces from the acid thrown on them back when they were on the force but their revenge must be and will be strictly in accordance with the letter of the law, ex-detectives, divorced people, lonely people, incredibly raventressed, silken slim-hipped hard-fucking/never-fucking beauties, etc. etc. Even an honest cop or two has done the right thing. And of course, the hard-boiled private dick.

There is plenty of ready psychology available to explain this phenomenon, too. People hardly ever see justice done in real life so they like to see it in fiction, is the most common explanation. The rest of it is just mindless entertainment. And there's nothing wrong with either, I'm thinking. It's just that I'm tired of being a part of it. The literature that has resulted from this one little sociological problem is sinking my brain, right here in this porn theater, on a sunny day in California. And, while we're on the subject, just how *is* Martin Windrow going to react to being sodomized by a portable whale with AIDS?

By now the camera has pulled back on the blow-job and we have the interior of an apartment. Behind the sweating couple is a window, and in the window, we can see, is a lovely view of the San Francisco Bay, with just a hint of the north tower of the Golden Gate Bridge in the far background. After some simple triangulation, we can see that this blowjob is taking place on a beautiful, clear day, high atop Russian Hill. Moreover, as the camera moves clumsily from one static angle to another, with only one subject in 'mind', we notice that this apartment is rather a well-appointed one. There's quite a nice pseudo-Flemish tapestry to one side of the window, beneath which are a lamp and a table most definitely designed by Mies van der Rohe, displaying a gorgeous ashtray of hand-blown glass with a roach clip in it, atop a copy of *Architectural Digest*. Things are heating up now in the foreground, between us and the decor, the guy, who is on his back with a pillow under his ass, quite naked, has placed his hands on the skull of the nude lady hovering over him, and begun to squint as he gyrates his hips into her face, so that she violently engulfs the entire and of course not-inconsiderable-by-your-and-my-standards length of his cock, accompanied by sounds not incomparable to those of a laundromat in a singles neighborhood on a Monday night.

After a lingering not to say infinitely long close-up of this action, during which the camera has a very difficult time keeping its subject within the frame, we get another medium shot, from a new angle. He's going to come, you can just tell it, and he does, all over her face, which must surely be two of the most difficult things required of porn actors, taking it out like that, taking it in the face like that, humping it all the way to the bank, some people are just naturally talented, I guess. And that thought is idly recurring to me, when I see that there is also a large bookcase in this well-appointed apartment, beyond the twitching couple, against the wall on the other side of the lovely view. With no more ingenuousness than as if I were actually in a bookstore, I tilt my head to one side, to browse the spines beyond the endless come shot. Wilhelm Reich, Huysmans, Burroughs—Edgar Rice and William S.—, Lenny Bruce, Hemingway, Beardsley illustrations, Henry Miller, *A Man With A Maid* by Anonymous, *Charbroiled Exeunt*—that's an Amber Twilight title. These are some literate Russian Hill dwellers here, I'm thinking . . . Then *Lady Chatterley's Lover*, *The Bell Jar*, *Delta of Venus*, *The Story of O*, a long row of Nero Wolfe mysteries . . . and—what's this? About six inches of Martin Windrow titles. A first edition of *The Gourmet*—and the second edition of it! Then *Ulysses's Dog*, *So Long, Pockface*, *This World Leaks Blood*, and *Squeam with a Skew*, *Heart of Mercury* . . . What? Wait a minute. I haven't even *written* that one yet. Come to think of it, *This World Leaks Blood* has been written, but it's not *published* yet—is it? I squeezed shut my eyes and opened them again. The bookcase was now out of the shot. The girl in the movie was cooing over her boy's performance, licking the tip of his cock and trying to get her tongue far enough out of her mouth and around the corner to get at a rivulet of sperm sliding down her cheek, and there's laughter in the theater . . . .

SIX

Every writer's dream. How interesting.

I could no longer think. But the laughter. The whole theater was laughing. *I* was laughing, too, it was true, but I had a reason, I was going insane and intended to enjoy myself. But the whole theater? What did they know about BOOK.SUB? Were they an embodiment of the Moral Imperative? Was my conquest of the banal to be paid off in turpitude-awareness therapy? Was some shit-for-brains author out there somewhere orchestrating this whole scenario? *I* am the shit-for-brains author around here. But even as I stood in confusion, the laughter subsided, and I saw an ostensible reason for it. A couple in the balcony had evidently forgotten themselves, and were fucking passionately against a wall. Apparently they were heterosexual. He, standing, supported her by her buttocks. She clasped her legs around his hips and gripped his shoulders. The entire audience turned in their seats or stood to take in this scene. It was indeed remarkable, if only on account of the degree of lust expressed by it, but in point of fact not much different from what was supposed to be on the screen. This was a penetration scene. People were half in and half out of their seats, looking uncertainly backwards. I turned and looked at the screen. A different man and woman now made eyes at each other over cocktails, in a different apartment. Generic EZ rock suffused their inane dialogue. Glasses clinked, the camera pulled back. A huge bookcase loomed behind them. I quickly averted my eyes. I looked down. Some kind of fluid, leaking along the sloped floor, gleamed in the darkness. The man and the woman grappling in the back of the theater screamed mutually, and the audience applauded. The man, staggering beneath the weight of the woman wrapped around his hips, and the necessary exertion, sagged with her against the wall. She, leaning her head back, made long, sweeping strokes along his back and his head with her arms and hands. I stole a glance at the screen. The scene had changed to a bedroom, and the man and woman of the previous shot were removing each other's clothes. No shelves of books were in sight. My eyes lingered gratefully on the simple tableau of a man and woman undressing in the banal privacy of their own home. Their bedlamps matched. The room was paneled in a natural wood stained beige. A huge, primary-colored football-player-catching-a-pass poster, framed in chrome, hung directly over the bed, between the lamps. The bed linen was carefully made up, with a red quilt on top. The message, when it flashed in the lower left hand corner of the screen, caught me unawares.

(xsub active) . . .

This dirty wink was much more obscene than anything going on in the movie. I fled the theater.

The street was horribly bright. I donned my shades. People drifted past me slowly. A small old woman, with swollen stockinged feet that twisted out of her sandals, and a tattered kerchief tied round her head, smiled at the young man exiting the pornographic theater. Her face was brown as a walnut and wrinkled as dried fruit.

"Ja get off?" she croaked, and pointed a crooked finger at the doors through which I had just exited. Her head did not come as high as my chest, and there wasn't a tooth in it. She laughed. I recoiled and hurried down the street.

Several doors from the theater there is a bar, a relic of the old neighborhood, called the Shoe Inn. Narrow and dark, it has none of the glossy blond oak appeal of the newer places up and down the street, and serves no Perrier, but you can get a beer and a shot for a dollar sixty. Martin Windrow drinks there, when he's in the neighborhood.

I hadn't had time to think yet. Even as I downed and chased a shot, *This World Leaks Blood*, broken into tiny virtually undetectable files scattered about the deepest recesses of the Crow Mignon computer, waited for the opportunity to piggyback another job, to sneak into the computers of Pre-eminent Printing, Milwaukee, Wisconsin. There to lie in wait for similar opportunities to publish and distribute itself. Good. A 50,000 copy first edition of so-called quality trade paperbacks @ $4.95. I'd make at least $500. Sell them all, it's more like twenty grand. Wonderful. But it's not published yet. This operation had started to mean serious money for everybody, whether they knew they were involved or not. Were my nerves going? Larceny ceases to be a misdemeanor and becomes felonious after the first $500, does it not? What would I get? Eight years? Five? Ten? Would I, like Jean Genet before me, be content to manufacture sabots by day, and cover my head with my blanket, at night, to savour the puissance of my own digestive tract? Cast amorous glances over the iron-pumping denizens of Death Row, during the fifteen minutes of mandatory daily recreation? No. I'd go berserk and perm my hair within a week.

So this was the Moral Imperative. Nasty.

The bar was nearly empty, but two or three of the regulars were there. I'd never spent enough time in the place to achieve this dubious status, and in fact preferred my anonymity. The catbird seat, hard by the front door, was empty and I took it. Next to me sat a woman who had lost her larynx and half her tongue to cancer, yet insisted on continuing to smoke unfiltered Chesterfields. Her vocal chords had been replaced by a marvelous mechanical device strapped across her throat that enabled her to talk by making a buzzing that modulated in pitch just enough to make her intelligible to people who were used to it. Further down the bar sat a red-faced Irishman nursing a screwdriver. He was the bartender due to begin his shift at four o'clock. Beyond him a tall man stood, hard by a glass of whiskey. The current bartender also had a drink, which he kept out of sight beneath the bar.

I hadn't yet had time to think.

In a way, to write a detective novel is an academic nihilism. It is to admit that while the only way to change anything is to change everything, to act is to change nothing. To signal complicity in this is to reiterate that only what has gone before will come after. No one is capable of understanding anything else—they don't want to. To comprehend these few simple axioms—which, like 2+2, or indivisibility by zero, are as inexplicable as they are irrefutable—and to deliberately violate them, is to domino your efforts into another universe, wherein you discover that you, like everyone else there, must hold a second job. It is on this second job that you, like everyone else, will devote all your efforts to the proposition that 2+2=4. If you demonstrate this complicity all week, every week, they will give you money. If you do not, they will make your life . . . difficult.

As this familiar canon recurred to me, I had been about to remove my sunglasses. I kept them on, but muttered aloud, agreeing with myself.

"Really," I nodded, turning my glass in the pool of beer at its base, "really . . . ."

The tall man at the other end of the bar had been staring at me. Now he said, "You're one of them," and turned to the others and said, "He's one of them."

"Thanks," I said. "Do *you* think 2+2=4?"

"Who says 2+2=4?" the woman with half a tongue buzzed.

"The IRS, for one," the tall man said.

"Sonofabitch," the woman said, "they're always right."

The man in the middle raised a pedagogical index finger and said, "One is truly free when one has learned to respect the rights of others."

I raised my glass. "Semper fiduciary."

Everyone took a drink in silence, followed by a resentful pause.

"So," said the thin Irishman, setting down his glass on the end of the bar while eying the woman, but addressing me. Though his hand shook noticeably, his tone was conversational. "You're one of these Romans we been hearing about?"

"Cancer," the mechanical larynx buzzed, tapping the back of my hand with her forefinger, "although lately here they've taken to calling 'em Moon Children."

"That must about explain it," said the bartender, replacing his drink under the counter.

"Not really . . . ," the woman rasped. It seemed that any sentiment she wished to express required her voice to mount a certain threshold of energy in order to sufficiently vibrate the mechanical device installed in her neck. This made wistfulness a violent act. Her second disability caused her to spill vodka on her blouse. The bartender gave her a white napkin with a red motto printed on it. *If you can read this, you drank it all.* She dabbed it at her chin and chest.

The tall man at the other end of the bar shifted the stare to me. "What do you do?" he said.

"Leave him alone," said the woman.

The tall man shrugged and held his glass to his lips. "I just thought maybe he left his seeing-eye dog outside."

"Would he want some water?" asked the bartender, solicitously.

"A round for the house," the tall man said.

The barman smiled. "Of water?" This got a laugh.

The Irishman turned his head away from the tall man and alternately patted and smoothed the bald spot on the back of it with the palm of a shaky hand. "Sure and always catchin the wave of his mind," he said demurely, "is me Jimmy."

I knew this bar as a good place for Windrow to be drinking in, and in fact had used it several times already. But so distracted was I that at first a rather unsettling thought had not occurred to me. This was that, in fact, in using this place I had made up several characters for the detective to talk to. One of them had been a woman. It had been a long time ago, perhaps as far back as *Ulysses's Dog*, or *So Long, Pockface*. Eight or ten books, each sufficiently indistinguishable from the other that details get mixed up and forgotten, recycled and confused. A problem with forgettable books. But this woman, had she not hennaed her hair, suffered from cancer, smoked Chesterfield cigarettes?

My new beer and shot arrived. "Thanks," I said, and toasted the tall man. He returned the gesture silently and sipped his new drink, a whiskey and soda. The Irishman received a new screwdriver, as did the barman, and the woman next to me soon had a second vodka rocks to back up her unfinished first one. Vodka rocks was what the woman drank in . . . *Squeam with a Skew?*

"My name's Jas," I suggested to her, and held out my hand.

"Myra," she rejoined immediately.

My hand went dead in hers. The name recalled the fictional incident to me. Windrow met a woman called Myra in this very bar in *Cable Car to Hell*, after he found the hanged sailor in the Seaman's Chapel at Fisherman's Wharf. The sailor had been the single thread to tie a nefarious pederast real estate magnate to a series of bath house murders being kept under wraps by the police for fear of a panic in the gay community, and had been wearing women's underwear under his sailor suit. So far so normal. I strained to recall what I could of the conversation ensuing in the bar. At the time of the writing, I'd only visited this bar a few times, and never actually seen a woman in the place, let alone a woman called Myra, with hennaed hair, and drinking vodka on the rocks. Then I remembered another detail. In the course of their conversation, Windrow had asked Myra why she was throwing down so much vodka at ten o'clock in the morning.

"Body's got cancer oughta keep a heat on," she had replied.

But she had no half tongue, no mechanical larynx.

And, as with the fictional Myra, the real Myra now volunteered some information.

"Cancer," she said, touching a disk of scar tissue on her throat the size of a silver dollar. I must have been staring. She opened her mouth and an angular appendage darted awkwardly out, a quarter of it missing. It looked like a cutaway illustration in an anatomy textbook. "Got my tongue, too," she buzzed, rather helpfully, holding out a Chesterfield. "Got a light?" The bartender reached between us and flicked a lighter before I could mutter that I didn't smoke, adding, as if diffidently, nor was I thinking of taking it up.

The other patrons stared silently at the bottles behind the bar and thought their own thoughts.

"You still smoke?" I blurted incredulously. "Didn't, I mean, don't cigarettes have something to do with ... cancer? Aren't they, ahm, related?"

"So they say," the woman buzzed, exhaling smoke. "Don't much matter to me, though. Nobody's keepin me warm nights."

"Now Myra," the bartender began.

"You shut up, Joe," she buzzed sharply. "Why should I quit? I lived a good life."

"That's true," said the tall man at the end of the bar, with a queer look in his eyes. "That's true ..."

"But Myra," Joe began, "it ain't like it's over ...."

The woman smiled and I glimpsed a handsomeness in her features that I hadn't noticed before. She sipped her drink. "It was a good one, wasn't it Mike," she buzzed.

"Aye," agreed the tall man, "that it was."

"Don't ye be gettin Irish on me now," said the Irishman between them with a wink over his drink at me. I smiled weakly, in an attempt not to betray the vertigo flirting with the contents of my stomach. For I was beginning to suspect that I had *made up* the woman sitting next to me. At the time I had endowed her with the ridiculous but catchy detail of being an inveterate chain-smoker who wouldn't quit smoking in spite of the fact that she had cancer. Now, several years later, here she was, apparently quite real, in an acute state of decrepitude well advanced from that in which I'd abandoned her, the moment Martin Windrow had walked out of this bar. But that had been *in a novel*. Not *in a bar*.

I experienced no sense of panic or despair or fear, such as I might have expected. Quite the contrary. A warm sense of community pervaded the bar. The sun came in the window at my back. The waterfall on the Olympia sign continued to cascade silently. A fly tentatively inspected the edge of the pool of beer widening around the base of my glass. All in all, there seemed to be a warmth about the place that I could only compare to the one I experienced when browsing deep within ... within ...

Within the memory banks of the huge Crow Mignon computer.

Things slowed down inside the Shoe Inn, as if my circuits, beginning to recognize the inevitability of a collision, had filled my veins with noradrenalin. A certain ocheroid tinge suffused the air. This was not altogether inconsistent with the normal atmosphere of the place. On the contrary, it made me feel as if I fit in there less awkwardly.

I looked curiously at the tall man. And who was this fellow who seemed to have shared tender moments with Myra, ostensible figment of my imagination? Had I conjured him up too, only to have forgotten? I could not place him. What a brutal godling I must have been, to have discarded these characters only moments after breathing life into them! To have abandoned them to the cruel courses of the utilitarian devices only whimsically and momentarily installed, for the purposes of getting Windrow from one page to another, from the last murder to the next, from the lousy neglected shelf one level up from the floor to the tacky evanescent glory of a dump near the cash register! *Heart of Mercury* indeed!

"Dear Mike ... ," the woman buzzed sentimentally, and a tear gleamed in the tall man's eye. "You were such a fool in 1955."

"Don't despair, Myra," smiled the bartender. "Some things never change."

I hastily threw a five on the counter and hurried out of the bar. Two blocks east I entered the newsstand and found four Martin Windrow books among the pornography and romance titles in the back. *Cable Car to Hell* was one of them. Sure enough, inside was a sequence I barely remembered having written.

When next he looked up, Windrow saw he had walked about two miles from the Seaman's Chapel, all the way along the Presidio, past Fort Mason, Gas House Cove, the Marina Green, to Fillmore, and a couple of blocks down Fillmore to Chestnut. He turned into the first bar he came to—and left immediately. As with the second and the third. These were all highly polished oak places, hung with ferns, bound in brass, mostly uncurtained glass on at least two sides, with double doors standing open to the bright sunny air. Not his kind of joints. He recalled the Sea Witch, a few blocks down, a few doors up from the second and probably last remaining seedy influence on this entire side of town, the Presidio Theater, representing that interesting residual phenomenon of the nineteensixties, pornography for nice people.

The Sea Witch was a narrow, dingy place, there was a catbird seat right against the door as you came in, with about twelve tarnished chrome and tattered red naugahyde cushioned stools making their way down the bar towards the single bathroom at the back. Beyond that there had once been a narrow galley, now gone, and the space left behind was piled high with cartons full of new and used long necked brown bottles of Hamm's, the only beer they served in the Sea Witch. You could always count on no more than three or four regulars being there, unless there was a wake someplace later on, when the place would be full. Not many of this kind of people lived in this neighborhood in San Francisco anymore. Windrow wondered if many of this kind of people lived anywhere anymore. A middle-aged lady held down the catbird seat, with plenty of makeup so badly applied it looked like her lips were out of focus. As Windrow sat to her left the bartender, a man with many miles on his face, squinting against the smoke rising from his cigarette, dropped an icecube into the lady's drink and covered it with a generous slow pour out of a bottle of Popov. Then he set the bottle on the bar between them and lit her Chesterfield for her. A tall man stood at the far end of the bar. He had a cigarette in one hand and one foot up on the rail, and he stared deep into the mirror beyond the bottles behind the bar. All the gestures, all the moves in this place seemed as if they had been rehearsed for the cabaret scenes in To Have and Have Not, *forty years before, and were now endlessly being reenacted—parodied—by an aging company of geriatrics with time on their hands and nothing else to do but perfect their stagely business, while they quietly drank and smoked the day away. It was the kind of joint that opened at six a.m. and had a few customers right away. All of them would be home in bed, quietly smashed, by three or four. A second shift would sift in about noon. These would be domesticated by sunset, dark at latest. Unless there was a wake someplace. In which case they all would still be there at nine, seriously drunk, talking blarney, and the joint might get crowded.*

Apparently there was no wake today. Only one other customer was in the place. He was an Irishman, short, with thin hair and a nose swollen by drink, who now appeared from the direction of the bathroom and took a stool at the bar in front of a screwdriver, midway between the seated lady and the standing, tall man.

It was Windrow's kind of place . . .

There they were, all four of them, slightly younger. I checked the copyright notice on the back of the title page. 1984.

Windrow took the stool between the woman and the pay telephone to the left of the door. "Bushmills, with a beer back," he said. The bartender retrieved an icy long neck and stood it on the bar.

"Buy Myra the drink," the tall man said, swaying slightly. "Fella too." He slurred his speech a bit, and Windrow could see the man had a pretty good heat on, for ten o'clock in the morning.

"Aw let the fella buy his own drink, Mike," the woman next to Windrow rasped, and she smiled at Windrow. Her voice was a jagged mass of sound, made up of spikes and jolts of frequencies that struggled through some unmentionable thicket in her throat, between her lungs and her mouth. It sounded like the old woman was on intimate terms with all the whiskey and cigarettes in the Marina District. Either that, or someone had kicked her in the throat. Windrow couldn't decide. It didn't seem like the joint was that rough . . . .

Her throat was intact! Damaged, but intact . . . .

But Windrow didn't give it that much thought. The memory of the young sailor's blackened tongue, how it had swollen in his mouth and forced its way out between the dead man's clenched teeth during the night, of the smell of death in the room, that overwhelmed even the pungency of the salt air and creosote and rotting barnacles from the underside of the pier, that seeped up through the floorboards of the chapel dedicated to the memories of sailors lost at sea, these would not let him yield his fullest attention to the matters at hand, not even to the shambles of a case that had started out yesterday so simply; let alone to the drunken man at the end of the bar, or the ruined larynx of the woman beside him. It was all he could do to choke down half his shot, then the rest, and follow it with a swallow of beer. But that seemed to improve things a bit . . . .

"When, Myra?" the tall man croaked, watching his image in the dark mirror behind the bar.

"Oh, Mike . . . ," the woman chided.

The tall man cleared the bar in front of him with the side of his hand. The glass shattered against the wall next to the bathroom and fell to the floor in pieces. The barroom became very still. The tall man continued to watch the mirror, and spoke very quietly. "When they going to cut it out of you, Myra?"

The woman picked up her drink and held it to her mouth. After a pause she said, "Take it easy, Mike, it's just a little cancer."

A nerve worked along the line of Mike's jaw.

"They'll get it all out in a day, and I'll be back in a week," Myra added gently, but loudly. It seemed that any sentiment she wished to express required a certain a threshold of energy in order to sufficiently vibrate what was left of her larynx, to get some coherent sound out of it.

Precisely the observation I'd made only moments ago!

The tall man's teeth were clenched. "And if they don't, Myra?"

Myra took a sip of her drink and placed it carefully back down on the bar. The bartender parked one foot on the rim of the sink beneath the countertop, and carefully, deeply inhaled through his cigarette, his fingers poised nearby, waiting, as it quivered in his pursed lips.

"Why then," Myra rasped, watching her fingers turn her glass in the pool of moisture that had condensed down its sides, "why then I guess I won't be back, will I . . . ?"

"Hey, buddy!"

"Ah," the bartender said, dropping his foot to the duck-boards on the floor beneath him, "what's all this about, anyway? Myra ain't goin nowhere. Huh? Are ya, Myra . . . ?"

"HEY, goddammit . . ."

I looked up in a daze. The proprietor, a huge, unlit cigar sticking out of his face, glared at me from behind his glass counter. "Can't you read, bud?"

I looked around. There was nobody else in the store. "Who? Me?"

"Yeah! You! Who the fuck—." He impatiently removed the cigar from his mouth and jabbed it in the direction of a hand-lettered rectangle of shirt cardboard taped to the edge of a shelf teeming with pornography, a few inches from my nose. "'Absolutely No Browsing!'" he yelled, quoting the sign for me, "Says right there, absofuckin-lutely no browsing. You buyin that goddamn book?"

"Buying, what, no, I wrote, I mean I . . . think I . . . have read it already . . . ." I sputtered to a halt, completely at a loss, for once, for words.

"Then put it back," the man said. "No browsin the skin mags."

"But," I began, showing him the cover, "this isn't . . . ."

"Sez you," the man sneered. And he prized his upper denture off its gums with a pop, displayed it on the tip of his tongue, and replaced it with a lascivious smack.

I looked at the cover myself. It was pretty sleazy. Not bad, really. I'd nearly forgotten the tableau of a runaway cablecar trailing severed nude limbs of mangled gender into the yawning maw of a berserk Tenderloin. At the time I had complained about it to the publisher who, with malevolent relish, as if taking pains to polish the round-ness of my education, informed me that if it weren't for the great expense lavished by himself on cover art, books such as mine would scarcely justify their existence, let alone that of their author's.

Or, wait a minute, maybe it was the cover of *The Gourmet* I'd complained about?

Maybe, by the time *Cable Car To Hell* came out, I'd learned my lesson? After all, by the time *Cable Car to Hell* came out, *I* was the publisher.

Absently, I replaced *Cable Car to Hell* in its slot on the rack.

"Sorry," I murmured.

"Shhe . . ." the news vendor said. He replaced his cigar in his mouth, leaned back against the edge of the seat of his stool, and resumed his perusal of the *Police Gazette*.

So Myra had made it back from the hospital after all, I was thinking as I left the store.

SEVEN

Get completely drunk
    Fall into a pit of nerves
        Wake up somebody, somewhere else.
    Change 'Martin Windrow' to 'Palmer Dendron.'
    Engage plum blossom speculation . . . .
    Create a genealogical chart of all the characters I've ever written. Show how they're related, which books, and multiple appearances, etc. Include a system of asterisks [*] to show whether I made them up or stole them from real life. Use a cross [†] to indicate whether or not they've been killed off. Create extensively indexed appendices to detail and census methods of liquidation, time of day or night (duration if excruciating), location, whether or not Mercury was in retrograde, etc. List murder weapons.
    Distill wine from the plums.
    You don't distill wine. One allows it to ferment.
    Download latest exotic modem software from user group's electronic bulletin board.
    Upload Martin Windrow fanclub info, with genealogical chart and appendices. Publish and market it as a Concordance. Compuserve?
    Actually, have you ever seen a real private detective? He's probably about thirty-two, maybe even younger. He has a beard and mustache, and they're neatly trimmed. He wears a sweater vest and wool pants to keep from freezing 'to death' in the San Francisco fog. His hair is done every morning with a hair dryer, carefully razor-

cut and styled every two weeks, no matter what. Bundles of keys and loose change tend to fall out of his pockets because of the semi-stylish cut of the pants. He chews on the ends of pencils and pens, these instruments are all over the place and readily show this abuse, but he can never find one that works when he needs to jot down a suspect license or phone number. Just last month he was busted by a uniformed cop for running a red light and couldn't talk his way out of the ticket. All in a day's work, he half shrugs and drops the pencil, but he ran the light in hot pursuit of a guy he'd been trying to get a line on for three weeks, who'd run it right in front of him and got away with it. Is that right, says the uniform, neatly clipping driver's license, registration, and proof of insurance to his ticket book, all in a row. Wait right here, sir, while I put you through the computer, just take a few minutes, no back talk, thank you, sir . . . . Didn't get the license number of the car either, the cop says over his shoulder as he walks back to the idling cruiser, tsk.

He's left fuming at the wheel, aw double-D gosh darnarootie, danged rotten ironic twist of the if it waddnt for dumb rotten he wouldn't have no *guignon* at all, not a-tall . . . . Hits the horn ring with his fist, the horn honks and he winces, checks the uniform in the rear view mirror, who glowers from under the visor, the underside of the visor lit by the glow from the screen of the DMV computer, the radio squawks, and our dick slides slowly down in his seat to wait for the ticket.

The next time you see him, this real detective, he's in the all-day mandatory driving school, to erase off his license the points he's otherwise going to get for running the red light. He's just given up trying to get any sympathy from the instructor or the rest of the class, who were amused by his story for a few minutes, but it's the same as everybody else's—they're all innocent—and anyway they would rather watch the educational film on cocaine abuse, starring a much re-habbed movie star. Our detective is left to chew on the end of a pencil, fitfully twisting the pages of the latest issue of *Psychology Today* in his lap, wondering how a convicted dope fiend can narrate a movie . . . show business . . . maybe that's the answer . . . . You think I'm kidding . . . .

" . . . *damn well the girl told you her whole dirty little story. We want to hear that story too, Mr. Windrow, every detail of it. We've had quite a few dealings with this little twitch in the past, and, frankly, I'm confident that if you tell it well enough Tiny here, even though he's a devout, I mean, dyed-in-the-wool fag, so that you can be assured that he'd scream bloody murder and call the cops on himself if a real female so much as showed him her tits, if you, as I say, tell the story well enough, Mr. Windrow, knowing our fourth party as well as we do, I'm fairly confident that it would be such a horny affair that Tiny here would get off all by himself. So that we can all see and partake of the splendid joy of it, yet remain uncontaminated."*

The thin, effete hoodlum sighed. "But if you don't tell it right, sir, why, he just won't be able to get himself off on it, and by the time you finish a pack of lies, or a short version that leaves out important details, well . . ." Thimbelina threw up his hands. "Well," he repeated, "I'm afraid he'll just have to take it out on you." He shook his head. "I won't be able to control him." He permitted himself a smile. "I might be forced into helping him . . . ."

Windrow could feel the sweat, beading up on his scalp in the interstices of his processed hair . . . .

Now wait a minute. We have the conventions, the mutual agreement between the author and the reader on certain matters of style, as laid out in the (unwritten) (hexadecimal) Hardboiled Bylaws. These, and the matter of big words. The detective does not have processed hair, o.k.? Get it straight. And never, ever, send your reader to the dictionary. He won't go. Not only that, he'll get pissed off at you because of his lack of knowledge. Moreover, the thought will absolutely not occur to him that it's *his* knowledge that's wanting, rather than your facility with the language. Surely, he will say, you uppity scrivener, there's a word containing fewer letters and syllables, approximately equivalent to 'interstices'? How does one pronounce that, anyway? It sounds like a brand of seatbelt for a race of spiders . . . .

I've tripped the Fag Flag in the Hard Boiled Bylaws. I forgot about it, or went too far, or no longer care . . . . Something . . . . At any rate, BOOK.SUB knows. When I return to my room the floor will be two feet thick in tractor-feed paper, covered with excoriations written at my own keyboard a scant two years ago . . . . BOOK.SUB will have rejected *Squeam with a Skew* in its entirety. That might have been o.k., but in dumping the book to disk on my computer the printer will fire up and list everything, the manuscript itself, the legal justifications, ticking off the appropriate Hardboiled Bylaws . . . . It'll all be there, waiting for Marlene's fireplace, and, later, the Rewrite and, ultimate bummer, Diminished Returns.

This particular Bylaw is real simple. It says, *Tough guys don't get sodomized.* That's it. And, *in extremis: Yea, even may they Pitch, verily they do not Catch.* Now, I wield enough economic power to get around some things. After all, I'm a member of the Mystery Writers of America, who subscribe to these unwritten laws. And, bottom line, I've made some money. But here I've gone a step too far. There's a corollary to the Sodomy Clause, and it's real simple, too. It says: *And if they do [get sodomized], they don't like it. No way. Ever.*

There are notable exceptions. Cain's *Serenade*, for example—although, look out, for here looms large ye Moral Imperative. A contemporary series, for another example, stars a gay detective, although, in fact, so far as I know, he cleaves, ahem, hard by the *extremis* corollary.

But the point is, even though festooned with all these conventions, these unshaven detectives got to look clean, morally, that is: they can be hygienically reprehensible (it's preferable), but their foe has to be morally inferior to them. They're carrying around more eponymous gear than a soldier of fortune . . . .

There he goes again. "Eponymous." Sounds like a phone booth on a planet of spiders . . . Greek spiders . . . .

So along with that, certain characters got to have ruined throats and cancer in their lives, to lend a certain amount of grit to this hallucination folks like to snuggle into and get thrilled by, while flying coast to coast or waiting on Death Row, like having a certain amount of sand in your salad means it's organic lettuce, or something . . . .

I mean, you've never even questioned Marlene's existence have you? In fact, aren't you just coasting along in here, waiting for me to get back to the house and be raped by Marlene? Or Tiny? Now there's a real guy . . . . That immense cock of his looks like the bowsprit of the *Flying Dutchman*, heaving out of the gloom of the seedy Tenderloin hotel room . . . . You can hear the squish as he strokes the fantastic length and thickness of the far end of his viscera . . . .

Viscera. That's eyewash on the planet of spiders, just hold it up to your face with your pedipalps . . . . Well don't forget the *octoculars*, too, godammit. You know, binoculars for spiders? Eight eyepieces, eight lens tubes, four focus knobs . . . Jesus Christ . . . .

But to have deliberately given her cancer, then forgotten about it, only to run its course in her helpless body . . . . Had no one thought to get her to a doctor?

The first thing was food. Yes, food. I grabbed a taxi and motored to North Beach, thinking all the way over there about how Hemingway, when he had no money, would describe in his nascent novels and stories fantastic meals in wonderful detail, to slake a hunger that ultimately would be satisfied beyond his wildest nightmares. I, possessed of so insignificant a talent, could afford to eat a huge Hu Nan meal at Brandy Ho's. Sweet and sour dumplings in a delicious ginger sauce sprinkled with chopped peppers and garlic, stuffed with a paté of pork and vegetables. Hot and sour beef, with sliced carrots, garlic, and onions, served over steamed rice. Cold noodle salad, with huge bean sprouts, plenty of slivered chicken, slices of raw, fresh cucumber, covered by a peanut sauce of extreme zest. Three Kirin beers. I skipped the smoked ham fried rice, with ropes of scrambled egg and fresh garden peas, likewise the carp, broiled whole and served on a bed of vegetables and rice, and segued directly to ginger ice cream with green tea, and ate the whole meal with my shades on. Absolutely No MSG. Meals with MSG are for when you have a deadline and the nightmares aren't forthcoming. But when you can eat like this, why write about it? Taking a post-prandial stroll up Grant Avenue, I saw many poets. Bob Kaufman, Gregory Corso and Kay McDonough with baby Nile, Neeli Cherkovski, Lawrence Ferlinghetti, Janice Blue all dressed in blue, David Moe, Jack Hirschman and Sara Menefee. While Kaye wasn't listening Corso told me I had no balls. Neeli told me he wasn't getting published. I discreetly refrained from telling him about BOOK.SUB. Without saying a word, Bob Kaufman said

My radio is teaching my goldfish jujitsu ....

Jack Hirschman read me one of the poems he'd written that day.

PEACEDOVE

Of the dove, of the
dove-lands and what they mean,
how it is
to be
a dove, a struggle-dove
the dove that's been born
over and over since
the end of the World War,
and where the dove comes from
and how it stands for
the utter
invincibility of peace
and is always triumphant
as the sincerely innate
inspiration of human beings.

At the time Jack hated electricity, so I knew he'd eschew anything as electrifying as BOOK.SUB. And all I could think about there on the street, with my full stomach, and hungry gentle poetic friends, was that I hadn't killed anybody yet today. But I had seen someone I'd maimed. This did not throw off my digestion. Instead, I got drunk and fell into a pit of nerves, woke up as some-body, somewhere, else. A pseudonym. So now, was the question, could the Moral Imperative yet seek me out? Of course. This is just a detective novel. I'm going to get mine, right in the kisser, from the sword of the Avenger, whoever she is. Would it be the lady with the ruined throat and tongue? Or would Tiny get to Windrow before he expired from AIDS? Does he really have AIDS, or is Thimbelina just smarter than Windrow? How about that woman who never got skinned in *The Gourmet*? Would somebody be selling pieces of me with Velcro fasteners on Fisherman's Wharf? How would it come? When? Should I get BOOK.SUB's by now not inconsiderable legal DO loop to make out my literary estate to Marlene?

Marlene. Right then, right there, in front of a dive called The Saloon on Grant Street, I resolved that never, ever, would I use the beautiful Marlene in a book. Stay just as you are, baby. Let your life take its natural course. Fuck your tenants as they come and go, collect their rent, forget them when they leave, keep a clean house. I'll never lift you, whole or in part, out of your quiet if somewhat adventurous little life next to Alta Plaza Park, and use you in a detective novel, so help me god. And I weaved down and around the corner, through the milling, frightened tourists, a bum or two, a poet/hooker, a saxophone player, a barker, to Carol Doda's Condor Club, at the corner of Broadway and Columbus. There, on the side of the building, is an ersatz California Historical Marker, commemorating the Condor as the Original Site of the Invention of Topless Dancing, if you care to believe that, and, placing one hand over my heart and the other on the plaque, I knelt on the sidewalk and repeated my solemn oath, aloud.

Someone charitably dropped a handful of coins between me and the wall.

But even as I so swore, my heart froze beneath the palm of my hand, galvanized into arrhythmia by a current that shot between it and the brass plaque. Hadn't I, somewhere, just last year, in *This World Leaks Blood*, or was it *Through a Mandible, Delicately*, or . . . . But hadn't I, just last year, used Marlene's pussy in a particularly grizzly scene? Just her pussy? Yes, I had, but it was in *Heart of Mercury*, a horrible scene, in which a young Oedipal Adonis had received his mother's pussy in the mail. It was sent to him by an insanely jealous rival for his mother's affections who, failing in his advances, had succumbed to the temptation of torturing and killing the woman, in order to deprive the rest of the world of her charm and affection. It was an unfortunate thing, a thing I deeply regretted doing, so deeply that, immediately upon completion of this very arduous piece of writing, so complicated in its ramifications that I sat up all night finishing the book, yet so real to me as I created it that my keyboard and cashmere sweater and chair seat were wringing wet with perspiration long before I was finished, that I immediately availed myself of the consolation of the real thing, even though it was three flights up and four in the morning, to assure myself that, (a) she was still alive and intact, and (b) it was as good as I remembered, and wrote, it. She was and it was and we were all so very young then . . . .

But it had been so necessary, borrowing Marlene's vagina, to the solution of the case. When the son opened the box containing the horrible discovery, there necessarily had to be a detailed description, absolutely lurid and convincing, for verisimilitude. Really, I outdid myself. In the course of things I had to restrain myself from running upstairs to make a detailed inspection, so as to get everything just right. But I knew that would lead to a cul de sac, so far as the novel went, and stuck to the task at hand, only later paying the visit. And, as the Moral Imperative would have it, this vicious act led to the unraveling of the perpetrator's otherwise unconnected but nonetheless stealthy and heinous butcherings, which had stymied Windrow and half the finest minds of the San Francisco Police Department for nearly two hundred pages....

The words of my oath died on my lips. Would Marlene's vagina go the route of Myra's tongue and larynx? Had I been innocently littering the city with ruined minds and bodies?—Innocently? *Venally!*—And, and what about my own penis? Had I not used my own penis in dozens, if not hundreds of fuck scenes? Had my mercenary practices insured that I contract, sooner if not later, herpes, syphilis, dismemberment, gonorrhea, three or four rapacious strains of venereal disease, as unidentifiable as they were incurable, urethritis, warts, impotency, AIDS itself? Would some sadist with sharpened canines and one eye soon slake his hunger with a grilled penis and cheese sandwich? Still kneeling against the wall I opened my fly and made a careful inspection. Still there, unpoxed. But even as I picked my teeth after dinner, somewhere in the back of my mind I planned to go home and write

The thin man shrugged. "Stretch Windrow's asshole," he said to Tiny. "And make it last!"

How could I do other than use my own asshole as a model, in a stretch of the imagination? I'm not going to bitch about violence in our society. It's always been here, it's always going to be here. It's the violence in my mind that bothers me.

Then it becomes a matter of an ice pick. Or perhaps an adze. Versus a chair leg or a splitting maul, nine pounds.

Asleep in your bed. 3:45 a.m. The house creaks. Moonlight pours through an open window. Shadows move in the stairwell. Was that a whisper? A footstep? A seagull lands on the roof with a distant thump. A raccoon makes its way through the ivy on top of the fence. It's chilly and you curl up in the bedclothes, for warmth. But that leaves your back exposed to the ice pick. The ice pick is very thin. It will penetrate the down comforter, the two or three wool blankets, your Tee shirt, your skin, musculature, the organ or perhaps bone beneath. The organism, your body, will scream and writhe around the wound before trying to twist away from it. The ice pick makes a very small puncture, so it will be necessary to strike very accurately, or many times. These in turn require absolute cool, or complete frenzy . . . .

What if I'd *had* the MSG?

. . . a fortunate thing for the victim if the first blow misses the vital organ or artery, and lodges in bone, a rib or clavicle. The undoubtedly determined force directing the initial strike ensures that the instrument, once lodged in bone, becomes very difficult to remove quickly, for the next thrust. This the victim can turn to his advantage. Even asleep, one may react. Screaming may help, but the chairleg under the bed is a better idea. Crush the wrist of the assailant, possibly disarming him. Likewise his skull. In any case, if the ice pick remains lodged in the victim, the assailant, disarmed, ironically becomes the target of his own violence. For the victim, stabbed, will not rest until he has pulped his oppressor, and likely will continue to rain blows long after the culprit has died . . . .

Or sushi . . . ? What is the aggression quotient of sushi?

The screaming can be a problem. Is this a rural or an urban kill? They will have planned accordingly . . . .

I wake up in the middle of the night, or half wake up, and there it is. The shadows are there, the house creaks, the seagull lands on the roof and I twitch so violently my back goes out. I'm so exhausted from failing to avoid Marlene when I came in that I nod out in spite of my terror, and the whole scenario blossoms in my mind like a flower of blood in a foetid syringe . . . .

Removing the ice pick is best left to the hands of skilled personnel.

If the weapon of choice is a burnishing tool, the wounds must necessarily give more trouble, as the three-sided puncture conforming to the silhouette of the tool will bleed profusely, and give great difficulty of repair, even to the finest surgeon . . . .

Where might Martin Windrow have seen that? How about a mimeographed handbook found in the drawer of a right-wing extremist?

The kind of mercy Marlene won't show me . . . I can live with that . . . She's not showing me mercy so she can show me some real mercy . . . But the scenarios, they leave me alone when she's outraging my sensibilities and, I must admit, sometimes I make advances on my own. Nothing out of line, you understand, nothing that might undermine the landlord/tenant arrangement. Never sleep in her bed, for example, snuggling up together would violate everything, show us both the kind of tenderness neither of us could stand, although, given her head, Marlene might like to go along with that . . . As the years go by she could gradually ease the tenants out, one by one, insofar as rent control allows, and put a child in each vacated room . . . Redecorating them first . . . I'd keep my room as an office and studio, for the computer and phone lines, a mail drop. Maybe take her name, too.

Get rid of Jas Jameson, detective writer, a name that bears the onus of years of fictional violence, of sexual outrage, and lately of fraudulent endeavors . . . .

A man gets tired. Tired of looking over his shoulder every time he goes out for the paper, tired of keeping a loaded pistol next to the cup of coffee on the arm of his favorite chair. Tired of keeping the volume down on the television, the stereo, the Sunday afternoon opera, so he can hear someone sneaking up on him. Tired of sending his little girls and his wife out of town at the least sign of trouble. Tired of forgetting what name the signatory is supposed to be on the check he's signing. Tired of looking out for the guy that's stronger than he is, tired of trying to second guess the weaker and stupider ones. Tired of winning all the time, knowing he only gets to lose once. Tired of resolving everything with violence, tired of bargaining with muscle. Tired, tired, tired . . . .

I come home a little drunk, on me it looks tired. The Plymouth is still parked up the street, a shadow in the passenger seat. The yellow Mercedes is gone. The Moral Imperative. Marlene is in the parlor on a big Victorian sofa reading *Vogue*. She's on her belly turning pages, her legs up in the air waving idly back and forth. The lavender house dress with yellow flowers . . . . There's a thin-stemmed glass of red wine on the rug nearby. I am tired. Her strawberry hair with the blonde tail and the violet eyes and the absolutely clear complexion . . . . Here lay a woman whose husband decided he was gay and left her, it took her years to get her self-esteem back. Even though she knew better she could not refrain from blaming herself, and he, married to the most beautiful woman he'd ever seen, whom he loved in fact, he was too confused to help her, he couldn't even help himself, he could only follow his desires, and these led him far, far from her arms, or the arms of any woman. This is a tough thing for anyone to take. It's worse than divorcing an asshole you made a mistake with, and more complicated than deserting someone you love for someone you love more. No matter how enlightened, the loved one abandoned in favor of a change in gender suffers greatly from a profound sense of inadequacy, compounded by their sense of loss. Marlene's been working on it, and she's coming along nicely. She has the advantage of being attractive, which has brought her plenty of experience in dealing with the vicissitudes of love—translated, this means that all men are assholes. We've been working on that. Compassion is the key. Compassion, time, and realism in the matter of resisting her charms. I go into the parlor and sit on the edge of the sofa. She continues to read. The hem of the dress is high up her thighs and she caresses my cheek with her toes. Her ass is irresistible, it curves up and away from her thighs beneath the dacron of the dress, but she's been resisting advances from me on that score, she never liked the idea of sodomy, and now that her husband has gone fag, even though it's been two and a half years, the suggestion makes her suspicious, and she balks. But Marlene is a passionate woman . . . . I need to do some research . . . . I run the palm of my hand along the nodes of her spine to the top of the low back of her dress and find the tab of the zipper there. I push my hand further until my fingers tangle in her blond tail and massage the base of her neck. She drops her head and turns against my hand. My hand comes back down her spine and brings the tab of the zipper with it. A V opens along her back, and the flesh is warm to the touch. The zipper stops just at the base of her spine and I rub her there. She drops her knee off the couch and puts her foot into my crotch.

Her behind begins to move off the couch, she's face down in *Vogue* now, making little sounds as she breathes. I lift the hem of her dress. Her ass is exposed, her cunt below it. Ah good, I think, it's still there, intact. I cup her vulva with the palm of my hand and she moves against it, my fingers cover her clitoris, separate the lips, my thumb finds her anus and she puckers up, as if giving a kiss, and the tip of my thumb slips in . . . . Now my other hand has found her breast and nipple, she crushes a cosmetics advertisement in her fingers, the telephone rings in my room upstairs, and I insert a finger in her vagina. It's very wet. I lubricate the outer lips by moving the finger in and out, in and out . . . . The thumb goes in a little more, the nail disappears, the first knuckle, and I hear the modem upstairs taking the call. Now Marlene has twisted around and is pulling at my belt. She has my cock in her mouth and upstairs the printer goes to standby with a barely audible tweet. She's voracious, I arch against her mouth and substitute my index finger for my thumb in her anus, she does not resist. On the contrary, she moves her hips in a circular motion that helps the ringfinger enter as well. The thumb finds her clitoris, the forefinger her cunt, my wrist is killing me. *Vogue* hits the floor. Her teeth rake my foreskin. The printer upstairs tweets loudly and begins to print. I pull my cock out of her mouth and enter her cunt, from behind. It's still intact, it's still perfect, it's a reason to live. I'm grateful and relieved . . . . She shouts and thrusts against me, nearly throwing me off the couch. I grip her hips and dig in my heels, holding on for my life. The woman comes almost immediately, long before I'm ready, with a scream. Time passes, we work at it, then she comes again. We're out of practice, we need to spend more time together. Sweat has appeared on my forehead, a bead drops off my nose onto her back. Marlene drops her head with a groan to the cabbage rose cushions, and raises her hips in the air. Below me I can see her asshole, I can hear it whispering to me, here, stupid, it's saying, put something here, it puckers come-hitherly. I pull my gleaming cock out of her cunt and place the length of it between the cheeks of her ass. I slide it back and forth, and wonder if I'll ever last long enough to get it into her, this is all rather exciting. But I'm hesitant, I don't want to risk all the progress we've made. Not for a mere thrill . . . . As if reading my thoughts Marlene reaches behind and places the tip of my penis against her anus. Even though the printer upstairs is a dot matrix job, very fast, still it's printing madly. Somebody's downloading a large file into my system. She presses the tip down, and thrusts her behind upwards. It's tight. She quickly removes her hand, spits into it, and brings the spittle back. She moistens the tip lovingly, taking care that the points of her nails don't scratch too much, just a little . . . . This is a thing not to be rushed, but pressing down the length of my cock and raising my hips lets the head slip in. Marlene groans and strokes the remaining length. I try to move the tip in and out a little bit, to get her used to it. The printer pauses for a form feed, which advances the paper to the next page, and starts to print again. Then Marlene encircles the base of my cock with her thumb and forefinger and pulls the entire length of it into her ass in one long, slow glide. Reverse peristalsis. Look it up. We groan together, as if we've heard a bad pun. She digs her nails and teeth into the arm of the couch, with her other hand she pulls at my scrotum. I cannot make it last, and quickly I'm hunched over her back, buried in her ass, saddling her entirely with my weight, both hands clutching at her breasts, sighing and coming like a repressed priest. Marlene comes again, with a little help from her hand, and we yell together. The telephone downstairs begins to ring. We ignore it. After awhile it stops ringing.

"This is a triumph of therapy," I tell her. "I pronounce you cured of all emotional maladies."

"Mmmmmmm . . . ," she coos, and buries my face in her hair, and bites my shoulder.

"Let's get married," I say cozily, into her hair. "I want you to make an honest tenant out of me."

"Oh, darling," Marlene says, "it'd be too beneath me, marrying one of my tenants. What would the girls next door say?"

"They charge by the half hour for this sort of thing I believe," I suggested, "and think you're a fool for not doing the same."

"That's a good idea," Marlene said thoughtfully. "I can't believe I never thought of it."

"I can't believe I suggested it."

A serious expression cast a shadow over her face. "Jas?" she said quietly.

"Yes, dear?"

"You didn't do that just because you wanted to, did you."

"Do what?"

"Ass-fuck me."

I was silent. The very sounds of the words in her lovely mouth caused nerves to twitch in my spent dick.

"Jas?"

I gave her my most incredulous look. "Are you mad? Do you know how good that felt?"

"How good?"

"Why, why . . ."

"You're a writer, come on: How good did it feel?"

"Why, well, er . . ."

"You see?"

"Wait, wait. I'm . . . I'm shy . . ."

"Shy!"

"Actually, I was wondering what that printer is up to."

"Well, you should. Nobody can trust a printer."

"No, no. The machine upstairs. Can't you hear it?"

She listened, then shrugged. "So? It's always sounding like that up there."

"But I'm not there."

"What difference does that make? It's a computer, isn't it?"

"Well, sure, but . . ."

"But so it doesn't need you to work, does it?"

"Why of course it does! Like any machine, a computer is only as good as the person who's running it. Without someone around to keep an eye on things, it would soon go off the rails . . ."

"So you say. It sounds to me like it's getting along just fine without you."

We listened for a while. Whatever was going on up there, form feeds and pages were flying over the platen, like pigeons in Manhattan. BOOK.SUB, looking after business. A 24-hour service.

After a time she asked me, "What's going on, then?"

"Beats me."

"Aren't you curious?"

I thought a moment. It seemed to me that in fact I no longer cared about what was going on upstairs. I felt as if that room up there belonged to somebody else. It was filled with someone else's books and electronics, and what went on there was no business of mine. I suspected that whatever went on up there, so long as it did not affect my life adversely, even were the activity profitable or nefarious, the less I knew about it the better off I would be.

The more I thought about this proposition the better I liked it. My distance from the room upstairs and its contents seemed to increase as I contemplated it. At length, I could hardly remember what it was that went on up there. I recalled experiencing the same feelings when I gave up television, in 1972. At first there was a feeling of self-loathing and disgust. Then a great emptiness over-came me, and I felt as if I had no purpose in life. But grad-ually I saw that I could learn to do new things. I realized that I had made myself a great gift of freedom in the form of Time. And after that first minute of doubt and dread-ful introspection, I never looked back. Perhaps Marlene and I could strike a deal with the contents of the room upstairs. Perhaps we could close it up and just collect the rent. I looked around Marlene's Victorian living room. The cabbage rose wall paper, the walnut armoire, the sideboard, the sliding doors that separated us from the dining room, now open, the waxed dining room table, the cabbage rose couch, magenta, lavender and cream . . . .

I kissed Marlene on the lips of her mouth, some-thing I could not remember, to tell you the truth, having ever taken the trouble to do. I could tell right away this was a mistake, and kissed her again. Her lips were very soft, and currently displayed that fullness and color so peculiar to her features after sex, attributes I could dote on, I realized, for years to come.

"Of course I wanted to," I said gently.

She shook her head. "I don't believe you. If you really meant it, you could compare it to something. Isn't that what writers do, compare things with other things?"

"And find them wanting, no doubt."

"You see?" she pouted, turning her face away from me. "You didn't really want to. It's just some experiment you were conducting, to see what it feels like." She tossed her curls. "I'll bet that old detective of yours is about to get it in the ass himself, and that's why you decided to try it on me."

"How uncanny," I said ingenuously.

"You see? I was right! Oh! Men!"

"Marlene . . ."

"Go away!"

"Marlene, wait . . ." I took her in my arms.

She struck at me. "Leave me alone!"

"Marlene, it was wonderful! Spontaneous! I swear . . ."

"Don't swear!" she shouted. "Compare!"

"It, it was . . . ," I stammered.

"You see?" she slapped me. "You weren't even paying attention!"

". . . like . . . like . . ."

"Animal!" She slapped me again.

"Wait, it, it was like the Titanic, slipping safely through the North Atlantic night."

"Oh!" She socked me in the chest.

"How about, how about a volcanic cone, brimming with lava, rising for the first time through the surface of the Pacific with a hiss?"

"No!"

"Then, then it was almost as if we were making love for the first time, only to find out we are brother and sister."

"What!"

"It was like, waking up at dawn, face down in your back yard, naked with a hangover, and finding yourself completely covered with lavender ornamental plum blossoms."

"That's better."

"Can I stop now?" I asked timidly.

"No!" she shouted.

"O.k., o.k., it was like, it was like . . . . It was like . . . ."

. . . It was like somebody drove a cement truck up his ass with the drum going and all thirteen yards in it badly mixed, heavy on the sand and aggregate, with new tires. But nothing that had ever happened to Windrow would stand up to being compared to it. He had been shot, stabbed and run over. He had been thrown off the balcony of a condominium, heaved through the plate glass window of a nightclub, thrown into the bottles behind a bar. A chandelier fell on his head in 1967, and the gas tank exploded when a motorcycle rear-ended his '69 Pinto in '78. Ralph Nader had been right about that car. That's what it was closest to, the gas tank going up on the Pinto. That, and being stabbed. That and, he hated to admit it, it killed him to admit it, he cut himself shaving in the morning, when he looked himself in the eye in the mirror and admitted it, but, after awhile, somewhere deep down inside, though he hated Tiny's guts, and would kill him when he found him . . . .

". . . it felt good, too," Marlene said coyly, quietly. Her tongue flicked over her lips. She lightly brushed the hairs along my thigh with the flat of her hand, so that they stood up after it passed over them. Then she said tenderly, "I wonder, if you'll let me suck you, I mean if you'll wash it off, and then if I suck you, can we . . . can we . . ." She blushed and lowered her eyes, then looked up through their lashes at me . . . and said . . .

". . . Can we do it again?" Windrow's eyes asked their reflections.

Or was it the other way around? Were the reflections asking their eyes?

Windrow left off shaving long enough to take a sip from the glass of dark Mexican beer with a raw egg in it, that stood on the shelf above the sink. His hand shook a bit.

Somewhere out on Folsom Street, below the open window of his office, a convertible stopped at a light. Its radio was loud. The tune was "You Can't Sit Down," by the Dovells.

Windrow listened for a moment, then set down his break-fast drink and continued shaving. Revenge on his mind, a razor in his hand. Goddamn twentieth century, *he thought to himself . . .*

Upstairs, paper spewed off the printer.

"Oh Marlene," I said softly, stroking her hair, "I'm so glad you're cured . . ."

EIGHT

The Fag Flag had tripped in the Hard Boiled Bylaws. I forgot about it, or went too far, or no longer cared. Something ... At any rate, BOOK.SUB knew. When I returned to my room the floor was two feet thick with tractor paper. BOOK.SUB had rejected *Scream to the Touch* in its entirety. That might have been okay, but somehow in dumping the book to disk on my computer the printer had fired up and listed everything: the communications, the manuscript itself, the legal justifications, the Bylaws, error codes .... It was all there, waiting for Marlene's fireplace.

The Bylaw is real simple. It says, *Tough guys don't get sodomized.* That's it. Now, I got enough power to get around some things. After all, I'm a member of the Mystery Writers of America, they wrote these unwritten laws. But I'd gone a step too far. There's a corollary to the Sodomy Clause, and it's real simple, too. It says: *And if they do [get sodomized], they don't like it.*

No way.

Ever.

(xsub active) . . .

Interview with Jim Nisbet by Patrick Marks and featuring Gent Sturgeon

One evening in the summer of 2010, Patrick Marks, the proprietor of The Green Arcade in San Francisco, sat down with Jim Nisbet and artist Gent Sturgeon, who did the cover of *A Moment of Doubt*, to nourish a few cocktails and chat about writing and other matters.

Patrick: So besides a wordsmith you are another kind of smith?

Jim: Well, I'm a cabinet maker, a carpenter, a construction type of guy. I've been doing it since I was a kid.

Patrick: You wrote *A Moment of Doubt* in the eighties. When did you last read it?

Jim: An hour ago, in a panic because I knew you were coming over. Actually, I last read it in the eighties, when I proofed and put it bed; probably around 1985.

Patrick: So where does that come in your oeuvre?

Jim: Good question. My first novel to get published was *The Gourmet*, in 1980. (Later *The Damned Don't Die*, retitled by Barry Gifford when he published it at Black Lizard in 1984 or '85). It was the old days: I sold the book and then two years went by before it came out. Galleys brayed off the pan of inked type, like that. In '80 I wrote a sequel, *Ulysses' Dog*, just in case *The Gourmet* rang the gong, you know. Outside chance, to say the least, but one feels that one must be ready. Stupid, too. What if it had actually happened? And then I girded my loins and wrote a novel that has never been published, *Jolan*, a "straight" novel. And then, caught between wavering and conflict-ing ambitions and a highly literate girlfriend, with whom I shared a suspicion of the detective novel, I wrote *A Moment of Doubt*. All three, note, might be construed as "Martin Windrow" novels. In fact, I was very disgusted by detective writing. It was too easy, it was too dumb, it was too clichéd. The first one I wrote twisted the clichés, the second one I wrote just pulled them out by the roots, and the third one gave it implants and extensions. Bottom line, *A Moment of Doubt* says, "I can't do this genre." And I probably could have been one of those guys, a Robert Parker kind of guy, not to denigrate Robert Parker—

Patrick: So it all comes to a head in *A Moment of Doubt*.

Jim: It's that writer guy going nuts writing detective fiction. Going way nuts. And while he was going way nuts, I was having way fun. All of a sudden stuff was available to me that hadn't been available—satire, pornography, obscenity, social issues—fun!

Patrick: In the dedication of the book you mention, in 1985, Kevin Killian.

Jim: Kevin Killian is one of the very few who read the manuscript and he was very complimentary about it. It would be interesting to see if he remembers it that way, or at all, for that matter. The way I recall his reaction, 25 years down the line, is, he laughed his ass off. You might want to check with him on that.

Patrick: It's insanely funny.

Jim: Well, I was really constrained by the so-called clichés of detective fiction. I trashed them out—and then what? I had a precedent. I saw Chandler, one of the originals of the genre—but that was thirty or forty years before—and he just became this hopeless drunk, who had all this attitude about other kinds of writing and really couldn't stomach Faulkner and, to me, writers that are extremely important. Chandler's not important—he's fun, and he was good, but he was not important.

Patrick: What about Dashiell Hammett?

Jim: I feel that Hammett was imprisoned by what he invented, too. Have you ever seen an unfinished novel of his called *Tulip*? It's a hundred pages of dialogue between two guys sitting around a kitchen table. It's really good dialogue, too. But nothing happens. It doesn't go anywhere, and he can't figure out what to do—he doesn't have Nick and Nora, and Asta and gin fizzes and dead bodies. It's really sad.

Patrick: *Red Harvest* is brilliant. In *A Moment of Doubt*, it seems to me that the characters in the novel within the novel seem to be taken out of Hammett, in a certain way.

Jim: Sure, there's a goof on him—you can't get away from that stuff. It permeates the entire genre.

Patrick: When did *Lethal Injection* come out?

Jim: That was next.

Patrick: One of the main characters in both *Lethal Injection* and *A Moment of Doubt* is the needle. I wondered if you wanted to talk about that at all.

Jim: Oh, God. [We all laugh.] Sure. Have I been a junkie—no. Have I shot dope—yes.

Patrick: I wasn't going to ask you if you were a junkie, I—

Jim: I never was. I was never interested in a trip down that mineshaft.

Patrick: Beyond the personal, there is this object, the needle that threads its way through and over the text, like the eye in the *Story of the Eye*. *Lethal Injection* is the most 'needle-ly' book there is.

Jim: What happened to William Burroughs?

Patrick: I was going to mention William Burroughs. [Jim laughs] In *Cities of the Red Night*—

Jim: I never read that.

Patrick: I think that is his best book.

Jim: Really? Not *The Wild Boys*, not *Naked Lunch*?

Patrick: No. I think *Naked Lunch* is kind of a farce. A lucky accident.

Jim: I agree. And of course it is a farce.

Patrick: But I bring up *Cities of the Red Night* because it also has a kind of science fiction element that you also partake in—you forgot about that genre.

Jim: Hey, *Windward Passage* won the San Francisco Book Festival science fiction award! So now Barry Gifford gets to say, "Jim, that's great you won that award, but it's kind of too bad because I never read science fiction, so now I don't have to read you anymore." I doubt he's ever read me anyway. Well, he did publish *Lethal Injection*. And *Death Puppet*. And *The Damned Don't Die*. So I presume he read them. It [Black Lizard] was a small house so it's hard to believe you could get a way without doing that.

Patrick: I am reading *Windward Passage* right now and I can see the science fiction clement but it's—

Jim: Bogus. I got a letter from someone and they wrote, "This isn't science fiction this is social fiction." Is that like fiction fiction? Help me out, here.

Patrick: I think that your writing is about writing, so often. In *A Moment of Doubt*, the computer plays a big part—do you remember that?

Jim: Absolutely. The problem is CPM. Who remembers CPM?

Patrick: Tech nostalgia. You know, the first book from The Green Arcade is *Low Bite* by Sin Soracco, which was fun to read, for many reasons, but I like it for its eighties quality. And *A Moment of Doubt* is really an amazing time capsule, with the computer terms, the gender issues— and the fear and the fun. The tech thing seems very pertinent today.

Jim: Well, here's a story. I had a big pile of Stendhal books, and I knew the period I was after—the time he spent in Naples—he was writing about Naples. There was a point at which Stendhal stopped keeping his journals and started writing novels. It's all very interesting to me and I just fail to see how I could have figured that out by just being on the Internet, if only because a lot of what you find on Wikipedia and the balance of the swarming id that is the idernet is unreliable. Just like the real id.

Patrick: And it's also very truncated. People fool themselves—they're mimicking—

Jim: They're mimicking scholarship. They're writing their term papers and they're wimping—they get little factoids and they salt them in there and it looks like they know what they're doing. And it's acceptable. The knowledge is not deep at all.

Patrick: There is also this cognitive problem, which I have been thinking about and seemed to come into high relief with Bush being re-elected. It seems that in certain dialogues, if you expressed ideas out of the scope of the predominant discourse people would look at you like you were crazy: if they hadn't heard it already, it didn't exist.

Jim: It's like those Republican talking points. The Bush administration was so good at that. They developed a message, boiled it town to a tag line or two, and then they would not deviate. They'd have everybody in the administration on all these different talk shows saying exactly the same thing. To the point where the Republicans who wanted to believe it were mouthing it and even the *New York Times*, like Judith Miller—the snake in the woodpile—made it seem like they weren't reading their own goddamn newspapers. They're going with the administration's message—don't get me started.

Patrick: And short term memory is another truncation, as well as the response in print—.

Jim: There's a lot of shoal sailing out there. But books are always there to be had and always will be there to be had. I don't think books are going to be replaced in my lifetime.

Patrick: Well, one of the funny things about the Kindle, which may be doomed because of other players and platforms—

Jim: Because of Apple? Because Apple exists. [Laughs]

Patrick: Really. I was going to say that I can take this book [I pick a book from a stack on a small table in Jim's living room], this Ettore Sottsass book and you can lend it to me, and I can borrow it and I might even forget to give it back to you, and you might get pissed off—

Jim: If I remember.

Patrick: "Who did I give that damned book to?"

Jim: "Who did I give that book to after the third gin and tonic?"

Patrick: But, at this time, if you have a Kindle you can't do that.

Jim: You can't zap a novel, that you paid $9.95 for, over to your buddy's Kindle, not like you can "bump" your business profile. Which, after all, might be worth something to the guy who wants to vend you a single malt scotch or a time-share in Cabo, or something.

Patrick: He has to pay $9.95, too.

Jim: It's fucked. The whole copy ethic and ethos—you can dub direct onto cds some great Coltrane album or this fabulous Jim Nisbet interview and hand it off to Gent or someone, and no one's paying for anything. But there is a point at which you say, "Hey, I bought this thing in the store and it's my right to do with this thing what I want." Everybody knows the copy's inferior—which is now an unreasonable argument, because even the originals suck, by the way—mp3s and cds and such. The audio quality is so bad, it's discouraging. Maybe they'll solve that problem, too. It doesn't sound like vinyl. God, we do bitch and moan like FM radio in the middle of the night.

Patrick: Technology may save us, but it may not.

Jim: It's not going to save us; it's all petroleum based.

Patrick: Your old Coltrane albums certainly are.

Jim: At least they did something right with that petroleum.

Patrick: But I also wanted to mention that fact that in 2009 Amazon deleted copies of 1984 from some people's Kindles, albeit over a copyright issue, and issued refunds and that just seems funny that in the analog world, the equivalent would be a corporation entering your home, rifling through your bookshelf and leaving a $11.07 on your nightstand. What have we gained—what are we giving up?

Jim: On that note, well, another round?

Patrick: I must have another question for you. Yes, I wanted to ask you about genre writing.

Jim: You know literature is literature. But I don't want to say that about my own work—that's up to someone else. It's not that I am not aware of what I am trying to do. *Sanctuary*, for example, always struck me as facile, and not a little sleazy. Excepting the matter of scale—recalling that, when asked about Faulkner, Flannery O'Connor quipped, "Who wants to be standing on the tracks when the Dixie Limited comes through?"—there's a case to be made for *Sanctuary* being Faulkner's moment of doubt. But literature is literature, wherever you find it.

Patrick: I think that is true about other arts, like music. I don't care if its Richard Strauss or Little Richard, you know, what's good is good.

Gent: I totally feel that way about writing. In fact I'm delighted when a book bounces around—

Jim: —yeah—

Gent: —genre-wise. I haven't read your new one—

Jim: —*Windward Passage*.

Gent: The piece that you read at the event the other night, I assumed was a hallucination.

Jim: Actually not.

Gent: It's not? It seemed like someone was really loaded.

Jim: [Laughs] That's the prologue, and it's the only chapter like that. It begins that way but that character doesn't turn up again until much later in the book.

Patrick: The prologue is insane, sci-fi, almost like a Vonnegut sci-fi. I never really considered Vonnegut to be science fiction. Did you? Do most people?

Jim: No, he was fooling around with it. The early books like *The Sirens of Titan*. But then came *Slaughterhouse Five*—nobody thinks that's science fiction.

Patrick: But it has time travel and other planets and—

Jim: —Ice Nine and all that stuff. The name of the Grateful Dead's publishing company.

Patrick: *God Bless You Mister, Rosewater*.

Jim: Yes, I read all those back in the sixties. Then I stopped reading him. When did I bail? I know Dan Simon had a huge hit with him.

Patrick: *A Man Without a Country*. Occasional pieces.

Jim: He did some great stuff. Philip K. Dick, the same deal.

Patrick: Crossing genres. Where do I shelve this?

Jim: Under D. BTW, PK and I have the same publisher in Italy—I'm thrilled.

Patrick: Who is that?

Jim: Sergio Fanucci. Fanucci Editore. I'll show you some of their books. They want my entire list. Did I say I'm thrilled?

Patrick: I think that I would call Philip K. Dick science fiction.

Jim: Why not? But it's a narrow consideration. Philip K. Dick's entire list. Do you know how many fucking books that is? Fanucci also has an American writer named Joe Lansdale—do you know his works?

Patrick: No.

Jim: I don't either; but Dennis McMillan tells me that when Joe Lansdale is good, he's really good.

Jim goes to study and returns with some of his Italian editions.

Gent: Man, this [*Iniezione letale*] has a weird cover.

Jim: It is a weird cover, nobody gets it.

Gent: Well, it's the [lethal injection] solution, cooking away.

Patrick: Gent got it.

Jim: Yeah, right. And this is *Dark Companion*, which they changed to *Cattive abitudini*, which means *Bad Habits*. Now, I ask you. And after talking to several people I retro-actively understood that they did not get the astrophysical subtext of this novel. Which is too fuckin' bad. But it's a hit, so what can I do? "Jim," my agent said, "enjoy the ride." Are we not pro?

I take another of Jim's Italian editions and remove a strip of colored paper which encircles it.

Patrick: What do think of bellybands on books?

Jim: It's a fact of life in Europe. And actually, that's a quote from a *La Repubblica* article by a Strega prize winner. And who am I to complain? I was so mystified by the whole approach to the covers and then it's storming the country so I just go, "Fuck, you know what? Hey, it's their culture, they get it and I don't, moreover, they paid for the right to do what they want." [Laughs] If I were an artist, I'd get really uptight. As it is . . . . But another point: if your metaphors are getting in the way of a good story, you're doing something wrong—so maybe I really do know what I'm doing!

Patrick: I want to ask you another question about existentialism.

Jim: Oh, yeah, we never finish with existentialism.

Patrick: I'm curious about Jim Thompson, because he is the first author I read who was, I would say, terminal. There were characters with no redemption. There was absolute ruthlessness and the dead end—

Jim: Every time I have this conversation, which isn't that often—

Patrick: —which one? Which conversation?

Jim: You know, redemptionless writing, dead end writing, the end of the world. Where do you put something like *Absalom, Absalom*?

Patrick: That is interesting.

Jim: Jack Hirschman, and I'm not sure if he was skirting the topic or not, said he thought *Absalom, Absalom* was the most literary novel of the twentieth century. François Guérif [Jim's French publisher] and I just say it's the greatest novel of the twentieth century. Bar none, we both love that book. To me, it has a lot of that stuff going on that you are talking about.

Patrick: It does.

Jim: But speaking as somebody from the South, I've never really gotten why anybody from somewhere else thinks they get Faulkner. [Laughs.] But the French really seem to get him. And Jim Thompson too, for that matter. And James Ellroy. François gets all those guys.

Patrick: But what are these moments, existential, terminal or not, the burning family house, the corpse, what are these moments and how do we get there? We watched this movie, based on a book I never read, *The Friends of Eddie Coyle*—

Jim: —George Higgins—I met him. I have his last book, *Rat on Fire*.

Patrick: How is it?

Jim: Not very good; he was having a big problem with that. But then, I don't think *Eddie Coyle* is that good. And boy, do I get an argument there. From the people who've read it, anyway, which is not that many people. But, on the whole, people I respect. Aforementioned Guérif, for example.

Patrick: The film is.

Jim: I have the book if you want to borrow it.

Patrick: I don't need to read the book.

Jim: Aha! [All laugh.]

Patrick: What's interesting about the film is that where there was this thing that happened in screen writing where it was okay to have films with characters whose lives were just an absolute dead end.

Jim: That was the fifties, *Gun Crazy*, the B movies, the shadows imprinted by the Bomb on the walls of the fifties.

Gent: It came back, in the seventies version,

Jim: Version of what?

Gent: Of that despair, and the seventies version is actually real legit. *Shampoo* is another good example.

Jim: Where people usually end that noir story, although it's not ending, is that Lee Marvin movie that ends on Alcatraz—

Gent: *Point Blank.*

Jim: Yes. And it was color. And they dropped the conceptual ax at that, the pigeon found the little bit of mesh on the roof of its hole. But they can't bear to exclude that movie, so they include it in noir. But as usual with those definitions—noir...really the original thing was these two French guys—you guys published the book[1] [Gent works at City Lights Books]—who noticed these films coming

---

1 *A Panorama of American Film Noir (1941–1953)*, by Raymond Borde and Etienne Chaumeton. City Lights 2002.

over—the French film industry was destroyed by WWII and these movies were coming from Hollywood that were approved and maybe weren't doing so well here, blah blah blah, and they gave this amazing picture of American life and the despair behind the Bomb and everything. *Kiss Me Deadly*—there's another great movie that has nothing to do with the book—nothing, nothing, NOTHING! Mickey Spillane, man. NOTHING! Just the title. And it's an amazing movie. I mean, the answering machine alone—you remember the answering machine?

Gent: Fantastic—way sci-fi.

Patrick: Did you read *Nightmare Alley*? Book so much better than the movie—even with Joan Blondell.

Jim: We could go on—to me one of the better books is *Treasure of the Sierra Madre*. I love that book—and the end is so much better in the book, where he has been beheaded...

Patrick: Hey, Faulkner worked on that film—

Jim: You know who knows a lot about Traven, and is fascinated by him, is Barry Gifford. He wrote a big piece on him, and met his daughter who still lives in Mexico City, she showed him Traven's library, his typewriter ... He wrote this really good piece that he's never been able to get published in Gringolandia—nobody's interested. He got it published in Spain and in Mexico, though. In Spain and Mexico, they remember the author of *The Treasure of The Sierra Madre* and, maybe more especially, the so-called Jungle books. There's another one called *The White Rose*, which I've never even seen, let alone read. *The Death Ship*.

Patrick: These things seem go in cycles.

Jim: Traven's always been an outsider. First of all, he never wanted to be found. John Huston even thought the guy who appeared to pick up the check for the movie was a schill.

Patrick: But he seems to resurge every so often. And the publishing revs up and then there's this great interest, and then he disappears again.

Jim: Yeah, I remember, in the early seventies there was this whole edition of all these Traven books—

Gent: Now there are these new editions of all these Huxley titles, all repackaged—a lot of chrome yellow—bright colors.

Jim: Aside from the fact that one notes that Huxley has a couple of translations in the New Directions Anthology of *Fleurs du Mal* translations, 1955, you know, nobody's talked to me about *Brave New World* in a long time. In one of my books I postulated a sixties bookshelf in which the guy becomes nauseous reading the titles. [All laugh.] And you can name them. It's in *The Octopus On My Head*. And it turns out that the junkie who's collecting them up to sell at Moe's [Moe's Books in Berkeley] does so via his membership in a thing called the Sixties Book Club. Darrell Gray, the poet, used to do this. I remember he signed up for a book club and they sent him an OED as an introductory thing, the two-volume one with the slipcase and the little drawer with the magnifying glass, and he took it up to Moe's and flogged it like for fifty bucks. Then he moved. I shagged this story for my book, although, I finely stipulate, Darrell wasn't a junky, he was just impoverished.

Patrick: Have you read Simenon?

Jim: I've read quite a lot of Simenon. Let me tell you a story about Simenon. I'm in the south of France, in Frontignan, not too far from Sète and the Cimetière marin, where Paul Valéry is buried. So I'm in Frontignan for this festival and there are many stories—that's where I met George Higgins, for an exemplary coincidence. Anyway, there was a display there of Simenon artifacts, a glass display case about waist high. It had his typewriter.

It had a manuscript open to page 75, with some little red marks, and then it had a calendar of something like May 1953. And the calendar had 9 or 10 days x'ed out in black and then 3 or 4 days blank and then 3 or 4 days x'ed out in red. And then it had the published book, which was open to the same page displayed in the typescript. So, the days x'ed out in black were the composition days, the blank days were devoted to post-compositional whoring and drinking, and the days x'ed in red were what it took to edit the thing. Done.

Patrick: I love that.

Jim: Oh, god it was fabulous. All these sweating writers milling around with a glass of white wine in the Mediterranean heat, trying to figure out who at this event was important for them to schmooze, and by the way they should be learning some French, and here I was, as usual, with my nose up against the vitrine of greatness.

[Major laughter all around]

Patrick: I have read a lot of Simenon in the past years.

Jim: I like the stuff without his cop, the *romans durs*.

Patrick: *Romans durs*. Great.

Jim: Listen, I am a carpenter. I can look at this wall. I can tell you—actually I built this house, but let's say it's your house and it's the first time I've been here. I can tell you that that wall is original, it's balloon framed, sixteen inches on center, of rough-cut two by fours. I can tell where they are, where the blocking is, why it didn't have any insulation, where there's some plumbing, over here. I can just look at this wall, and I can see through it. And I have that problem with most thrillers—especially cop novels and detective novels. Until I get to someone like Robin Cook—Derek Raymond, who is so strong; or Patrick Manchette, who was so tricky and funny, and right on and doing the same thing, twisting all the clichés—and also being trapped by them. Manchette, I think, was as buffaloed by the whole thing as anybody. But getting buffaloed was not Simenon's problem, although he wound up all alone in a big chateau in Switzerland, old and rich and out of his mind. Like, uh, I can't think of his name—the only book I ever liked of his was *Stiletto*.

Gent: Harold Robbins.

Jim: Damn, Gent! Exact! Harold Robbins was taken off his yacht in Nice or Cap d'Antibes or someplace, semi-comatose on cocaine, gibbering to the ambulance attendants, who have had to strap him into the stretcher and speak no English, "Don't you know who I am? I'm the greatest writer in the world . . ." Out of his fucking mind. Have you seen a Harold Robbins novel lately? Gone. In the landfill. Munificent cash bovinity incarnate, those books, while he was alive. Sold millions. Poof.

Patrick: But we have wandered from you and your work. I think you are saved from these grisly fates by your incredible dark humor—in life and in your writing.

Jim: Humor, black, dark. Lucia Berlin, you may remember her, a great short story writer, and though she had a lot of trouble with alcohol her whole life, she told me once that in *Lethal Injection*, at that moment when the doctor pulls his truck into his yard, after the prison death chamber scene, in the beginning, after he puts down the inmate, he pulls into his yard and gently crushes the taillights of his wife's Mercedes. Then he gets out of his truck, and it's Texas, and it's night and there's all these stars up there, and the crickets are going, and he starts thinking about the stars and the crickets, and they say, he says to himself, they say that the breedle of the cricket, the frequency of the breedle of the cricket is directly proportional to ambient temperature, and is it possible to get so fucking hot that the crickets might explode? [All laugh.] Lucia said she read that and had to put the book down, she was laughing so hard. Because it seemed to her to be a really typical drunken chain of thought. Completely alcoholic, off the charts, drunken chain of thought. I wasn't necessarily thinking about it that way when I wrote it but—

Patrick: But you were so drunk when you wrote it that—

Jim: No. I go to writing at nine in the morning with a cup of coffee—I don't ever drink when I'm writing. I don't drink when I work—too many power tools. Including the mind. You can get hurt.

Credo of The Green Arcade
The Green Arcade, a curated bookstore,
specializes in sustainability, from the built
environment to the natural world. The Green
Arcade is a meeting place for rebels, flaneurs,
farmers and architects: those who build, inhabit,
and add something valuable to the world.

The Green Arcade
1680 Market Street
San Francisco, CA 94102-5949
www.thegreenarcade.com

ABOUT PM PRESS

PM Press was founded at the end of 2007 by a small collection of folks with decades of publishing, media, and organizing experience. PM Press co-conspirators have published and distributed hundreds of books, pamphlets, CDs, and DVDs. Members of PM have founded enduring book fairs, spearheaded victorious tenant organizing campaigns, and worked closely with bookstores, academic conferences, and even rock bands to deliver political and challenging ideas to all walks of life. We're old enough to know what we're doing and young enough to know what's at stake.

We seek to create radical and stimulating fiction and non-fiction books, pamphlets, t-shirts, visual and audio materials to entertain, educate and inspire you. We aim to distribute these through every available channel with every available technology — whether that means you are seeing anarchist classics at our bookfair stalls; reading our latest vegan cookbook at the café; downloading geeky fiction e-books; or digging new music and timely videos from our website.

PM Press is always on the lookout for talented and skilled volunteers, artists, activists and writers to work with. If you have a great idea for a project or can contribute in some way, please get in touch.

PM Press
PO Box 23912
Oakland, CA 94623
www.pmpress.org

FRIENDS OF PM PRESS

These are indisputably momentous times — the financial system is melting down globally and the Empire is stumbling. Now more than ever there is a vital need for radical ideas.

In the three years since its founding — and on a mere shoestring — PM Press has risen to the formidable challenge of publishing and distributing knowledge and entertainment for the struggles ahead. With over 100 releases to date, we have published an impressive and stimulating array of literature, art, music, politics, and culture. Using every available medium, we've succeeded in connecting those hungry for ideas and information to those putting them into practice.

Friends of PM allows you to directly help impact, amplify, and revitalize the discourse and actions of radical writers, filmmakers, and artists. It provides us with a stable foundation from which we can build upon our early successes and provides a much-needed subsidy for the materials that can't necessarily pay their own way. You can help make that happen – and receive every new title automatically delivered to your door once a month – by joining as a Friend of PM Press. And, we'll throw in a free T-Shirt when you sign up.

Here are your options:
- **$25 a month** Get all books and pamphlets plus 50% discount on all webstore purchases
- **$25 a month** Get all CDs and DVDs plus 50% discount on all webstore purchases
- **$40 a month** Get all PM Press releases plus 50% discount on all webstore purchases
- **$100 a month** Superstar — Everything plus PM merchandise, free downloads, and 50% discount on all webstore purchases

For those who can't afford $25 or more a month, we're introducing **Sustainer Rates** at $15, $10 and $5. Sustainers get a free PM Press t-shirt and a 50% discount on all purchases from our website.

Your Visa or Mastercard will be billed once a month, until you tell us to stop. Or until our efforts succeed in bringing the revolution around. Or the financial meltdown of Capital makes plastic redundant. Whichever comes first.

with PM Press
Low Bite
Sin Soracco

the green arcade

ISBN: 978-1-60486-226-3
144 pages $14.95

Low Bite Sin Soracco's prison novel about survival, dignity, friendship and insubordination. The view from inside a women's prison isn't a pretty one, and Morgan, the narrator, knows that as well as anyone. White, female, 26, convicted of night time breaking and entering with force, she works in the prison law library, giving legal counsel of more-or-mostly-less usefulness to other convicts. More useful is the hootch stash she keeps behind the law books.

And she has plenty of enemies—like Johnson, the lesbian-hating warden, and Alex, the "pretty little dude" lawyer who doesn't like her free legal advice. Then there's Rosalie and Birdeye—serious rustlers whose loyalty lasts about as long as their cigarettes hold out. And then there's China: Latina, female, 22, holding US citizenship through marriage, convicted of conspiracy to commit murder—a dangerous woman who is safer in prison than she is on the streets. They're all trying to get through without getting caught or going straight, but there's just one catch—a bloodstained bank account that everybody wants, including some players on the outside. *Low Bite*: an underground classic reprinted at last and the first title in the new imprint from The Green Arcade.

"Vicious, funny, cunning, ruthless, explicit... a tough original look at inside loves and larcenies." — Kirkus Reviews

"Where else can you find the grittiness of girls-behind-bars mixed with intelligence, brilliant prose, and emotional ferocity? Sin Soracco sets the standard for prison writing. Hardboiled and with brains!" — Peter Maravelis, editor *San Francisco Noir* 1 and 2

"Tells a gripping story concerning a group of women in a California prison: their crimes, their relationships, their hopes and dreams." — *Publisher's Weekly*

"Sin Soracco is the original Black Lizard. *Low Bite* will take a chunk out of your leg if not your heart. Read it, it will devour you." — Barry Gifford, author *Port Tropique*, Founder Black Lizard Books

from PM Press

Fire on the Mountain
Terry Bisson
with an Introduction by Mumia Abu-Jamal

ISBN: 978-1-60486-087-0
208 pages $15.95

It's 1959 in socialist Virginia. The Deep South is an independent Black nation called Nova Africa. The second Mars expedition is about to touch down on the red planet. And a pregnant scientist is climbing the Blue Ridge in search of her great-great grandfather, a teenage slave who fought with John Brown and Harriet Tubman's guerrilla army.

Long unavailable in the US, published in France as *Nova Africa*, *Fire on the Mountain* is the story of what might have happened if John Brown's raid on Harper's Ferry had succeeded—and the Civil War had been started not by the slave owners but the abolitionists.

"History revisioned, turned inside out ... Bisson's wild and wonderful imagination has taken some strange turns to arrive at such a destination." — Madison Smartt Bell, Anisfield-Wolf Award winner and author of *Devil's Dream*

"You don't forget Bisson's characters, even well after you've finished his books. His *Fire on the Mountain* does for the Civil War what Philip K. Dick's *The Man in the High Castle* did for World War Two." — George Alec Effinger, winner of the Hugo and Nebula awards for *Shrödinger's Kitten*, and author of the Marîd Audran trilogy.

"A talent for evoking the joyful, vertiginous experiences of a world at fundamental turning points." — *Publishers Weekly*

"Few works have moved me as deeply, as thoroughly, as Terry Bisson's *Fire On The Mountain*... With this single poignant story, Bisson molds a world as sweet as banana cream pies, and as briny as hot tears." — Mumia Abu-Jamal, death row prisoner and author of *Live From Death Row*, from the Introduction.

Lonely Hearts Killer
Tomoyuki Hoshino

ISBN: 978-1-60486-084-9
288 pages $15.95

What happens when a popular and young
emperor suddenly dies, and the only person
available to succeed him is his sister? How can
people in an island country survive as climate
change and martial law are eroding more and
more opportunities for local sustainability
and mutual aid? And what can be done to
challenge the rise of a new authoritarian political leadership at a time
when the general public is obsessed with fears related to personal and
national "security"? These and other provocative questions provide the
backdrop for this powerhouse novel about young adults embroiled in
what appear to be more private matters – friendships, sex, a love suicide,
and struggles to cope with grief and work.

PM Press is proud to bring you this first English translation of a full-
length novel by the award-winning author Tomoyuki Hoshino.

"A major novel by Tomoyuki Hoshino, one of the most compelling
and challenging writers in Japan today, *Lonely Hearts Killer* deftly
weaves a path between geopolitical events and individual experience,
forcing a personal confrontation with the political brutality of the
postmodern era. Adrienne Hurley's brilliant translation captures the
nuance and wit of Hoshino's exploration of depths that rise to the
surface in the violent acts of contemporary youth." — Thomas LaMarre,
William Dawson Professor of East Asian Studies, McGill University

"Since his debut, Hoshino has used as the core of his writing a unique
sense of the unreality of things, allowing him to illuminate otherwise
hidden realities within Japanese society. And as he continues to write
from this tricky position, it goes without saying that he produces
work upon work of extraordinary beauty and power." — Yuko Tsushima,
award-winning Japanese novelist

"Reading Hoshino's novels is like traveling to a strange land all by
yourself. You touch down on an airfield in a foreign country, get your
passport stamped, and leave the airport all nerves and anticipation.
The area around an airport is more or less the same in any country.
It is sterile and without character. There, you have no real sense of
having come somewhere new. But then you take a deep breath and a
smell you've never encountered enters your nose, a wind you've never
felt brushes against your skin, and an unknown substance rains down
upon your head." — Mitsuyo Kakuta, award-winning Japanese novelist

I-5
Summer Brenner

ISBN: 978-1-60486-019-1
256 pages $15.95

A novel of crime, transport, and sex, *I-5* tells the bleak and brutal story of Anya and her journey north from Los Angeles to Oakland on the interstate that bisects the Central Valley of California.

Anya is the victim of a deep deception. Someone has lied to her; and because of this lie, she is kept under lock and key, used by her employer to service men, and indebted for the privilege. In exchange, she lives in the United States and fantasizes on a future American freedom. Or as she remarks to a friend, "Would she rather be fucking a dog... or living like a dog?" In Anya's world, it's a reasonable question.

Much of *I-5* transpires on the eponymous interstate. Anya travels with her "manager" and driver from Los Angeles to Oakland. It's a macabre journey: a drop at Denny's, a bad patch of fog, a visit to a "correctional facility," a rendezvous with an organ grinder, and a dramatic entry across Oakland's city limits.

"Insightful, innovative and riveting. After its lyrical beginning inside Anya's head, *I-5* shifts momentum into a rollicking gangsters-on-the-lam tale that is in turns blackly humorous, suspenseful, heartbreaking and always populated by intriguing characters. Anya is a wonderful, believable heroine, her tragic tale told from the inside out, without a shred of sentimental pity, which makes it all the stronger. A twisty, fast-paced ride you won't soon forget." — Denise Hamilton, author of the *L.A.Times* bestseller *The Last Embrace.*

"I'm in awe. *I-5* moves so fast you can barely catch your breath. It's as tough as tires, as real and nasty as road rage, and best of all, it careens at breakneck speed over as many twists and turns as you'll find on The Grapevine. What a ride! *I-5*'s a hard-boiled standout." — Julie Smith, editor of *New Orleans Noir* and author of the Skip Langdon and Talba Wallis crime novel series

"In *I-5*, Summer Brenner deals with the onerous and gruesome subject of sex trafficking calmly and forcefully, making the reader feel the pain of its victims. The trick to forging a successful narrative is always in the details, and *I-5* provides them in abundance. This book bleeds truth — after you finish it, the blood will be on your hands." — Barry Gifford, author, poet and screenwriter

SWITCHBLADE **from PM Press**

Pike
Benjamin Whitmer

ISBN: 978-1-60486-089-4
224 pages $15.95

Douglas Pike is no longer the murderous
hustler he was in his youth, but reforming
hasn't made him much kinder. He's just living
out his life in his Appalachian hometown,
working odd jobs with his partner, Rory,
hemming in his demons the best he can.
And his best seems just good enough until
his estranged daughter overdoses and he takes in his twelve-year-old
granddaughter, Wendy.

Just as the two are beginning to forge a relationship, Derrick
Kreiger, a dirty Cincinnati cop, starts to take an unhealthy interest in
the girl. Pike and Rory head to Cincinnati to learn what they can about
Derrick and the death of Pike's daughter, and the three men circle, evenly
matched predators in a human wilderness of junkie squats, roadhouse
bars and homeless Vietnam vet encampments.

"**Without so much as a sideways glance towards gentility, *Pike* is one
righteous mutherfucker of a read. I move that we put Whitmer's balls
in a vise and keep slowly notching up the torque until he's willing to
divulge the secret of how he managed to hit such a perfect stride his
first time out of the blocks.**" — Ward Churchill

"**Benjamin Whitmer's *Pike* captures the grime and the rage of my
not-so fair city with disturbing precision. The words don't just tell a
story here, they scream, bleed, and burst into flames. *Pike*, like its
eponymous main character, is a vicious punisher that doesn't mince
words or take prisoners, and no one walks away unscathed. This one's
going to haunt me for quite some time.**" — Nathan Singer

"**This is what noir is, what it can be when it stops playing nice — blunt
force drama stripped down to the bone, then made to dance across
the page.**" — Stephen Graham Jones

SWITCHBLADE **from PM Press**

The Jook
Gary Phillips

ISBN: 978-1-60486-040-5
256 pages $15.95

Zelmont Raines has slid a long way since his ability to jook, to out maneuver his opponents on the field, made him a Super Bowl winning wide receiver, earning him lucrative endorsement deals and more than his share of female attention. But Zee hasn't always been good at saying no, so a series of missteps involving drugs, a paternity suit or two, legal entanglements, shaky investments and recurring injuries have virtually sidelined his career.

That is until Los Angeles gets a new pro franchise, the Barons, and Zelmont has one last chance at the big time he dearly misses. Just as it seems he might be getting back in the flow, he's enraptured by Wilma Wells, the leggy and brainy lawyer for the team—who has a ruthless game plan all her own. And it's Zelmont who might get jooked.

"Phillips, author of the acclaimed Ivan Monk series, takes elements of Jim Thompson (the ending), black-exploitation flicks (the profanity-fueled dialogue), and *Penthouse* magazine (the sex is anatomically correct) to create an over-the-top violent caper in which there is no honor, no respect, no love, and plenty of money. Anyone who liked George Pelecanos' *King Suckerman* is going to love this even-grittier take on many of the same themes." — Wes Lukowsky, *Booklist*

"Enough gritty gossip, blistering action and trash talk to make real life L.A. seem comparatively wholesome." — Kirkus Reviews

"Gary Phillips writes tough and gritty parables about life and death on the mean streets—a place where sometimes just surviving is a noble enough cause. His is a voice that should be heard and celebrated. It rings true once again in *The Jook*, a story where all of Phillips' talents are on display." — Michael Connelly, author of the Harry Bosch books